···LIMIT OF···
DARKNESS

The Solomons

BUKA

BOUGAINVILLE

Kahili
Moila Pt.
Buin Hr.
Faisyo
Shortland

CHOISEUL

VELLA LAVELLA

Vila Kula Gulf
Visurisu Pt.
Munda
Vanguku
Yaholi Bay

NEW GEORGIA

Rekata Bay

SANTA ISABEL

RUSSELL IS.

Esperance Sayo
Tulagi

MALAITA

Lunga Pt.
Henderson Field

GUADALCANAL

100 MILES

SAN CRISTÓBAL

E. HOWARD HUNT
LIMIT OF DARKNESS

STEIN AND DAY/*Publishers*/New York

This book is a novel. It is fictional and none of its characters represent, nor are they intended to represent, anyone living or dead.

In fulfilling the obligations of my agreement as war correspondent, I submitted the manuscript of this book to the War and Navy Departments.

The Review Sections of the War Department, Bureau of Public Relations, and the Navy Department, Office of Public Relations, have found no objection to the publication of this book for reasons of military or naval security.

E. H. H.

The song, "I've Got Sixpence," which appears on pages 128, 129, and 195, is used by special permission. Copyright, 1941, by Bradbury Wood Ltd., London. Copyright, 1943, by CHAPPELL & CO., INC., N.Y. Sole selling agent for U.S., Canada, and Newfoundland, MUTUAL MUSIC SOCIETY, INC., New York

FIRST STEIN AND DAY PAPERBACK EDITION NOVEMBER 1985
Limit of Darkness is reprinted by arrangement with the author.
Copyright © 1944 by Howard Hunt
All rights reserved
Designed by Stefan Salter
Printed in the United States of America
Stein and Day, Incorporated
Scarborough House
Briarcliff Manor, N.Y. 10510
ISBN 0-8128-8232-6

TO

THE MEN WHO FLEW

FROM HENDERSON

He who, from zone to zone,
Guides through the boundless sky thy certain flight,
In the long way that I must tread alone,
  Will lead my steps aright.

Bryant

LIMIT OF DARKNESS

THE SQUADRON

LIEUTENANT-COMMANDER LAWRENCE McRAE USNR:
Commanding Officer of Torpedo-Bombing Squadron Eleven
U.S. Naval Academy '32. Former test-pilot at Curtiss Wright. Divorced

LIEUTENANT JOSEPH CORDELL USN: *Executive Officer*
U.S. Naval Academy '35

LIEUTENANT ELIOT LANE FORSYTH USNR: *Ivy League*
graduate who became a naval aviator instead of going to law school

LIEUTENANT (j.g.) BEN LAMBERT USNR: *Survivor of the*
Battle of Midway

ENSIGN PARKER LEWIS USNR (Babe): *Youngest pilot.*
Recently married

ENSIGN GRIFFIN: *Replacement pilot*

STRIKE COMMAND

LIEUTENANT-COLONEL MANUEL SAMPSON USMC:
Staff Intelligence Officer

FLIGHT LIEUTENANT ARTHUR VAUGHAN RNZAF.
Former commercial flier. Now strike homing pilot

LIEUTENANT (j.g.) PAUL SCOTT USNR:
Aviation Intelligence watch officer

WAR CORRESPONDENT

FRANCIS X. O'BANNON: *Ex-printer's devil and night-court reporter*
Now representing a Washington newspaper syndicate

REMEMBRANCE OF
THINGS PAST

Miriam: Widow of one of McRae's classmates

Ann Robinson: Army nurse Lambert knew in Honolulu

Linda Chapin: Forsyth's girl on the boat

Marge: Babe's young wife

Jean Anderson: Lambert's girl on the beach

Morning

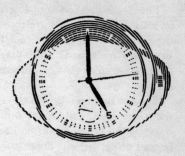

$\mathcal{T}$HE SUN OF THE SOUTH PACIFIC CAME UP SLOWLY OVER THE eastern tip of Guadalcanal in the Solomons. Its warm light touched the coral reefs and shallows of the little bays offshore, then crept along to the beaches and the jungle—awakening, disclosing, shadowing—its rays moving over the trees and the vines of the jungle peaks until they lighted the end of the bomber strip at Henderson Field.

Beyond the periphery of Henderson's great dusty oval, under the evenly spaced copra palms of the Lever plantation, squatted the tents of the men who flew from Henderson. Between their tents, dug into the coral and the loamy earth, were their foxholes. Strung between the tall bare trunks of the palms were wires and cords that held their damp, half-washed clothes. A breeze from the sea sprang up, stirring the limp laundry, swaying it, and then was gone into the green, dark jungle.

And, as the sun warmed the jungle, it killed the mists that had clung to it during the night. They lifted and died as they became transparent and harmless, and the birds shrieked their protests as they flew from tree to tree trying to escape the coming of the day.

3

The clouds that had hung low over Kokumbona, smothering its hills in layers of mist, retreated upward, leaving below on the grasses and the leaves a cool, heavy dew. Sealark Channel, between Guadalcanal and Tulagi Harbor, swelled a little as the tide began to change, glittering back at the pale morning sky.

The square green canvas tents of the men were damp with the night dews, and, as the sun rose, the slanted sides were warmed and began to steam. Each tent was alike except that, instead of packed dirt floors, the officers' had wood planking raised a foot or so above the ground. During the rainy season a man could never get dry because water flowed uninterruptedly across the ground under his tent, and in a little while the packed dirt turned to sloggy thick mud that deepened and thickened as the rains fell and men walked through it. But there had been no long rains for a time and now during the day there was only the dust, and, at night, the rats that ran across the ground and gnawed ceaselessly at your musette bag.

The sun always drove away the *anopheles* mosquito, and as long as there was daylight you could be fairly sure that any mosquito that bit you did not carry malaria. Instead, it was probably the *Aedes Egypti* that gave you dengue. As the dew evaporated from the outside of the tents, the interiors became hot and muggy, and men tossed in their sleep, pushing aside their blankets. When you did that it opened up the mosquito netting so that the flies could get in and light on your face and wake you or just buzz inside the sixty-odd cubic feet of netting-enclosed air.

Lieutenant (j.g.) Ben Lambert lay on his back staring up at the ridge pole of the tent, watching the bright flecks of light on the green canvas background where holes had formed in the sides. He had wakened, as he always did, when the first

4

Dauntless zoomed the field. He realized that it was morning and that he had not been flying the night before. Because he flew almost every night, he was surprised until he remembered that Weather had called off the strike. They had got as far as Strike Operations before the final reports came in, and then the skipper had said no go. He remembered riding back along the dark Lunga Point road, drunk with the relaxation of anti-climax, and then getting into his cot without even writing a letter. He was not yet enough awake to look around the tent and see where Joe Cordell was. Lambert closed his eyes and thought about going back to sleep, but the salty sweat stung and he opened his eyes again as the fifth Dauntless zoomed low over the palms and turned to the west, banking tightly to catch up with the others that were already forming up for the five-o'clock flight to Munda.

He lay in his cot and looked at the part of the tent he could see without moving his head. Around the sides, covering about three feet of the framework, stained cotton gauze was tacked to keep out insects. Above the framework, wooden poles ran upward at an angle until joined by the ridge pole. A cord hung down from the ridge pole holding at eye-level a large battery flashlight. Beneath the flashlight was a wooden table made from old ammunition boxes and covered haphazardly with dirty torn magazines. There was a candle stump stuck in an empty sparkling Burgundy bottle he had brought back from Australia. So far the rats had not eaten the candle, but he knew that one night they would.

Ben Lambert felt the sweat roll down his temple and drop off on the pillow beneath his head. He turned his face side-ways in order to blot off the other little globules that had formed on his cheek and lips, but the pillow was damp and did not absorb the additional moisture. The final effect was to coat his face with a film of sweat.

The screen door hung ajar and Lambert could see flies coming into the tent. He felt at the sides of his cot to find out if the netting was still tucked underneath the mattress, but his hands could detect no gaps. He brought back his hands, letting them lie parallel with his body on top of the damp mattress cover. Cordell moved in the cot a few feet away and the flies rose from the netting and buzzed angrily before alighting again in their interminable search for food. . . . Or was it the smell of sweat that attracted them? There was a seat beside the table, made from a metal bomb crate that had been cut in half. Where the green paint had chipped off, rust had set in so that whenever you sat down red oxide dust was ground into the khaki of your rump. No one had bothered to paint over the rust, and he knew that in time the legs would rust through where the paint had chipped around the rivets and some flyer would have a nasty fall. All of this would happen in possibly six months. Lambert turned his head a little more and saw that the bag of candy issued him at mess the night before had been gnawed by the rats. It had spilled onto the rusty green metal seat and some of the pieces had fallen to the floor. The bag was swarming with ants and he watched them climb up and down one leg of the seat in perfectly spaced trails that reached from the floor to the torn paper bag. He drew up his legs to cool his loins, and the flies on his netting buzzed. The ants continued to ascend and descend unhurriedly.

A Catalina, returning from a patrol up the Slot, gunned its engines as it made an approach from the far end of Henderson. Lieutenant Eliot Forsyth turned on his cot, throwing his arm that had been lying on his bare chest against the mosquito netting. He woke a little, hearing the fast swoosh of the Cat overhead as the pilot cut the throttles. A Catalina had a noise all its own when it came in for a landing. The engines backfired biliously with pistol-like explosions, and when the plane was past the last row of palms at the fringe of the strip, it settled fast to meet the soft dust of the field. Forsyth did not see those things happen, but visualized them automatically as he lay in his sack. He wondered whether to shave now or wait another day. The rash on his chin was clearing up where for a while he had sported a scanty blond Vandyke. He could feel perspiration smarting against the enlarged pores. Eliot moved his toes and felt the quick small pains that came where the fungus had eaten cracks in the skin between his toes. Today would be a good day to wash them in permanganate—if there was any. He was glad the fungus had not reached his ears the way it had McRae's. That was because he had not gone swimming off Lunga Point the way the others did when they first got there. For a while after you got to the islands, you compared every beach to Waikiki and then after a while you realized that Waikiki was pretty skimpy and littered and touristy, and the beaches that you flew over every day had more natural beauty and color than any in Hawaii. It was a holdover from the old easy life that made you bring the Beach Club complex with you wherever you went. When you finally realized that a beach in the South Pacific was not fundamentally a beautiful place to swim from or to play house near, but a wonderful spot to pull yourself up on from the water after you were shot down, you had achieved a great deal of maturity, and that in combat aviation was a highly desirable quality.

Eliot Forsyth brought his hand back through his close-cropped blond hair. It felt limp from the sweat of his scalp and he wondered if the sun would make him grow prematurely bald. At twenty-five you began to think of things like that, particularly if unmarried, and Forsyth decided that from now on he would always wear his baseball cap in the sunlight, even if he were only walking over to the mess hall.

The chair beside him had been made from an old potato crate, and his forty-five holster and his weapons belt were lying on it. The holster had turned so that he could see only the butt and the streak of rust running the length of it where the bluing and the oil had been rubbed away by friction with the side of the cockpit. Another inch on either side of a TBF cockpit would make it really comfortable.

The flat breathy roar of a Hudson taking off beat through the palms to Forsyth's tent. New Zealanders going out on weather missions, he knew. He looked at his gun lying on the chair beside his cot and thought that he would field strip it in the afternoon and take the rust from the butt. The early-morning breeze came through the tent, swaying the rawhide leg-thong that hung down toward the floor from the holster.

Joe Cordell heard the New Zealander's Hudson pass overhead as it turned to head up the Slot toward Bougainville. He rolled his tongue inside his mouth, over his teeth and gums, and regretted that he had stayed up so late drinking with Larry McRae. He did not particularly like to drink, but he and Larry were the only two Academy fliers in the squadron and, although Larry had finished ahead of him, Cordell felt that it was good to make the others aware of that old school bond whenever possible. He wondered where McRae had picked up that tremendous bottle of Schenley's. The bottle was about two feet tall and must have held well over a gallon. The original liquor had long since vanished, but the bottle was a kind of squadron trade-mark and the boys who flew back from Sydney or Suva or Noumea were expected to bring back enough to keep the bottle filled.

Cordell's khaki shirt was lying folded over the back of the chair beside him. It was bleached from the sun and constant scrubbings with laundry soap. His silver lieutenant's bars were spotted with verdigris and he felt resentment rise as he remembered the Jap in the Honolulu uniform shop who had assured him that they were solid silver. Cordell knew that if he polished the spots, the rest of the silver plating would wear off and the bars would be useless. He wondered why he had not brought more. The hell with them, he thought. In another month he ought to get his gold leaves. He'd sell the bars to Lambert or Flynn.

His heavy blue-steel beard rasped against the pillow as he turned his head. The sun was coming in through his side of the tent, making the muddy sidewall gauze translucent. He could hear men talking on the other side of the bivouac area as they walked to their tents. Probably P-boat pilots in from a search. He wondered if there was any more shipping in Buin Harbor. The Japs never let very many ships accumulate in their harbors. Two or three at a time were all you could find in the daytime, because they brought in a string of small boats and barges at night and had them unloaded and on their way north before dawn. Last night there had been only three ships off Buin. If the squadron went on the strike tonight he hoped there would be more. The Japs were getting damned handy with their searchlights, and at fifteen hundred feet the ack-ack seemed to fall around you like hail.

Cordell lifted his head a little as he heard a feeble splashing sound under the table. He raised up under the netting until he could see his bucket helmet under the table, two-thirds full of soapy water. He saw the surface stir and knew that one of the rats was still alive. He wondered how many had got into the trap during the night. From one side to the other, across the rim of the helmet, a flat piece of wood was balanced. A nail in either end acted like an axle, permitting the thin wood to spin freely above the water. Small pieces of cheese were clipped to each side so that the trap was self-baiting—and self-setting. A mouse or a rat started across the little bridge toward the cheese and then the axle would spin as the rodent over-balanced and fell into the water. Then it would swim frantically around inside the helmet, whimpering until it drowned in the soapy water. Joe Cordell held himself on his elbows and watched the water until there was no longer any motion.

Babe Lewis felt the rumble of the heavy bomb carriers as they moved down the jungle road from the bomb-dispersal area to the edge of Henderson near the ordnance shacks. He had fallen asleep wearing skivvy shirt and shorts, but during the night the shirt had begun to feel like a warm washcloth and he had struggled out of it. As he lay there blinking his eyes, he could feel the wetness of his shorts as they stuck to his thighs and the salt pain of *dhobie* itch in his groin.

He looked down the length of the cot, through the netting, and saw his blues hanging from a nail in the tent framework. There were streaks of green-gray mold on the back, and around the single ensign's stripe on the sleeve, a thick green fuzz was being nourished by the French gold lace. He wondered why he had brought them with him; at Ford Island they had told him to leave everything behind except his khakis. The heavy uniforms had been a millstone that stayed with him from island to island until they and he had reached the Solomons. Now they were done for. It made him a little sick to see the damp growths that made his uniforms look as though they had just been disinterred.

Babe lay motionless on his bunk, wondering if Forsyth were awake. He knew he did not rate being quartered with Forsyth, but he was glad to be with him. Lewis was the young-est of his class to get torpedo planes and now he was the young-est TBF pilot at Henderson. It worried him a little when he thought about it that way. The others had been at Midway or the Coral Sea, or had knocked out the Tokyo Express during the early island fighting. Babe had only been on two strikes so far, and he was glad the one last night had been called off. He knew he could not fly up the Slot every night the way the others had—not until he got used to the idea of dying. But he had promised Marge to come back and he would. . . . If you didn't think about a thing it couldn't happen to you. Babe would not think about not coming back. He had too much to live for—Marge and his family and going back to State for his degree when it was over. Babe wondered if he was going to be a father. The mails were so mixed up that he couldn't keep track of the letters that were sent, and Marge was too lazy to date them. She had said something in the last letter that made him think she was going to have a child.

In the stillness of the tent he began to feel desire for his wife. He lay on his cot, feeling lonely and very far away from her. When they were married he had never seriously considered the months or maybe the years he would have to spend away from her, and now that they were apart he kept telling himself, Oh, God, if I can just get back again without crashing or being killed by flak so that I can write and tell her how it is and that I think about her in the nights when I'm flying and dream of her in the afternoons when I'm sleeping. . . .

Babe felt the sweat under his jaws grow cold as he lay there wanting his wife, and then he turned his head when he heard Forsyth start to put on his shoes.

A Corsair banked and skidded crazily a few feet above the palms as it practiced strafing runs for the afternoon strike at Vila, and the heavy whine of its propeller overhead woke Squadron Commander Larry McRae. He lay flinching from the F4U's piercing drone until it was gone over Henderson, heading low over Sealark Channel. Lying on his back, with his head tilted forward by the bunched-up pillow, he could feel little fingers of sweat rolling down his face, reaching over his cheeks from his black curly hair. On his chest, the small rivulets lost themselves in the thick short mat, only to join again at his breastbone and flow together into the hollow of his navel. The only part of his body that felt cool was his back, just below the kidneys. His mattress cover was so wet that his back felt clammy. He opened his eyes slowly, feeling the heaviness of the lids. His head began to ache and he remembered that he had sat up drinking with Cordell after the strike had been called off. His tent was smaller than the others, but he lived in it alone. There was a wooden closet for his clothes that one of the mechs had made from an engine crate. The boy was going to paint it when he had been killed over Rekata Bay two months ago. Larry McRae could see that termite dust from the cabinet had drifted down on his sea chest. In another two months it would probably come tumbling apart like the Wonderful One-Hoss Shay and he would have to start out with a canteenful of liquor looking for a Seabee to make another.

His blue baseball cap lay on the table in the center of the room. Just above the beginning of the brim were pinned the miniature gold wings of a naval aviator, and above them, centered on the cap, the gold leaf of a lieutenant-commander. On the middle of the table was his big Schenley display bottle. He had got it in Buffalo, when he was testing planes for Curtiss-Wright, by breaking a liquor-store window one night after a bad day at the field. Empty or full, it had been with him for six years. He remembered how his wife had objected to it. Looking at it, he realized that it was only a little over half full. He wished Cordell had not taken so much. Cordell, he thought, drank like an Irishman, but never remembered to bring anything back when he went to Espiritu Santo or Auckland.

McRae turned on his side, feeling the mattress cover stick

to his body as he rolled over. The early morning sun hurt his eyes as it streamed through the screened doorway, and he turned away and saw on the table, beside his big bottle, the letter he had begun to write late last night. He could not remember what he had said in it, but after a while he would get up and read it over. He would probably have to rewrite it several times. His ear began to hurt again and he knew that the pillow would be discolored from the yellow discharge of the fungus infection he had got from swimming.

He was deciding what he should say in the letter when he heard somebody walking toward his tent. He looked toward the door and saw it was a Marine orderly from the communications hut. The Marine knocked on the door.

"Yes," McRae said.

"Six o'clock, sir," the orderly said.

"Thank you," McRae said. He sat up on the cot and started pulling the mosquito netting from under the mattress. It was almost time for breakfast.

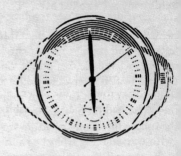

*L*AMBERT OPENED THE SCREEN DOOR AND WALKED DOWN THE three wooden steps outside the tent. He was wearing dirty canvas sneakers and a pair of bleached khaki shorts. There was a shelf nailed to the side of the tent framework and it held his and Cordell's shaving gear. Two bucket helmets lay on the shelf and, beside them, scraps of soap and old razor blades thick with rust. He took one of the helmets and held it while he tilted the spare gas can that held their daily water supply, water pumped from the Lunga River and partly purified. Each morning a young Marine came to the tent with a full water can and removed the empty one. You washed yourself and your khakis and shaved with it. Lambert held the can until the helmet was half filled. Then he brought the improvised washbasin to the shelf and began to wash his hands. One of the first things you learned was to rinse yourself thoroughly after having had soap on your skin. Otherwise, little serum-filled blisters broke out all over your hands, and it was a hell of a job to get rid of them. He emptied the dirty water and refilled the helmet. This time he noticed that the water was rusty from the inside of the can. He wet his shaving brush in

14

the helmet water and tried to work up a little lather on his face, but the water was too brackish. He stroked the shaving brush over his face until he had covered it with a thin layer of soap. Then he picked up his rusty razor, dipped it into the cold water of the helmet and began to shave.

Cordell came out of the tent with his toothbrush in one hand and a dirty towel in the other. His canteen was on his hip and when he had reached the washing shelf, he took it out of the canvas holder and dipped the toothbrush inside, wetting it with the chlorinated water.

There was a can of magnesia tooth powder on the wooden shelf. Cordell poured a little into his palm and covered the tufts of his brush with it. He stood away from the shelf and brushed his teeth, leaning so that the foam would not drip on his body. He felt the thick taste in his mouth leave as the acids were neutralized by the tooth powder, and he rolled his tongue around so that the solution could reach every part. His salivary glands were stimulated by the peppermint taste and he became thirsty. Finally he stopped brushing his teeth and rinsed his mouth with the canteen water. He drank a few mouthfuls and in the morning quietness he could hear Lambert's razor scraping against his unsoftened beard. He watched Ben grimace as he shaved the hollows of his neck, and decided that he would wait until after breakfast.

Lambert finished shaving and rinsed his razor in the helmet.

"How d'you feel, Joe?" he asked.

"Just fair," Cordell said. He took the other helmet from the shelf and began filling it with brown water from the can.

"Play crib last night?"

"No," Cordell said. "We just drank and talked."

"He's a good guy," Lambert said. "I like the skipper."

"He knows a lot about flying," Cordell said, beginning to

wash his hands. "He's got more hours than you or I will ever get."

Lambert took down his blue-striped washcloth from a nail and wet it in the helmet. He rubbed it across his forehead and then down his face on either side, taking off the slick feel of the shaving soap. He wrung it out and dipped it into the helmet again, rubbing his neck until there was no more soap on it. Then he twisted the water from the washcloth and hung it up on the nail again. A spot of rust had formed on the cloth where the nail touched it when it was hung the same way every morning. He walked a few feet away from the side of the tent and emptied the helmet on the ground, watching until the water had been absorbed before he took the helmet back to the shelf; it was easy for mosquitoes to breed if you left puddles. He wet his hands under the water can and ran them through his short black hair. The cool water felt good on his scalp and he rubbed it with his fingertips.

When he went inside the tent again he saw the ant-covered candy on the seat and picked it up. He opened the door with one hand and threw the torn paper bag out of the tent. It rolled on the ground and split open as it hit the base of a palm tree forty feet away.

Cordell looked up from his washing. "No more candy issued till next week," he said.

"That was stale anyway," Lambert said. He listened to Cordell's washing noises as he threaded his belt through his knife sheath, putting the tip of it in his right hip pocket so that it would be out of the way. Then he reached under his cot and brought out a pair of gray cotton socks. He took off his sneakers and began to roll them on.

McRae had shaved and was standing outside his tent feeling his clothes on the line. One shirt was almost dry and by noon the others would be ready. In front of the tent some wide planks led up to the door, and to the right of it was a sign:

VTB II

Lt. Comdr. McRae USNR

He looked at the sign as he went back into his tent. The R at the end bothered him. His application for return to the regular Navy was in the mill somewhere and he wished the designation would come through. Now that he was back in harness he might as well go whole hog. He stood in front of a camp mirror, trying to comb his thick black hair, but the curls fell back into place, making him look as rumpled as before. In the mirror he could see sweat stains starting to show through his shirt. McRae put away his comb and wound his wrist watch, looking at his unfinished letter on the table. His heavy Marine-issue shoes felt stiff on his feet and hurt his ankles a little, but he knew they would soften by the time he had walked to the mess hall. He turned to go out of the tent and as he passed the table he picked up the letter he had begun last night. It started: "Dear Miriam," and there was only a paragraph more. As he walked out into the morning sunlight toward the mess hall he tore the letter into thin strips and let them fall behind him on the grass.

Forsyth and Lewis were walking through the ankle-high grass between the palms when they saw the Squadron Commander tear up his letter.

"I wonder what that was," Babe said.

"Probably a memo to one of us," Forsyth said. "He makes a lot of notes and keeps them until he's memorized them. When he wants to spring them on us he knows exactly what he wants to say."

They walked over the little ridges between the palms, stepping over the old brown cocoanut husks and the small green ones that the wind had knocked down, until they were near the mess hall. It was a long Quonset hut with a shed built in back for a galley. A wisp of steam rose above the shed and they knew that there would be at least something warm for breakfast.

"Wonder what we'll have," Babe said.

"The usual, I guess," Forsyth said. "No ships in for a week."

Babe felt the heavy clomp of his shoes and the rasp of the longer grasses against his bare legs. He was self-conscious about the newness of his khakis. This morning he would wash them all, scrub them and hang them to bleach in the sun. He hated the thought of cutting the sleeves from the rest of his shirts, but it was too much trouble to roll them. He looked at the faded khakis Eliot Forsyth wore and wondered how long it would take to bleach his the same color.

They saw the skipper go into the mess hall and heard the light buzz of respectful good-morning-sirs that followed him down the aisle between tables. Babe held the door open for Forsyth and went in after him. He took off his blue wool baseball cap with the single gold bar and miniature wings pinned on it and held it in his hand until he came to his seat at one of the tables. There were ten tables in the mess hall, five on each side of the hut, seating ten men each. The mess was seldom full because most of the flights came at odd hours and the dive-bomber pilots who ate with them usually had a late breakfast after they got back from Munda or Rekata Bay.

Babe Lewis sat down on the bench in front of the wooden table. Several wide planks had been nailed together and placed over sawhorses. Tin plates and stainless-steel knives and forks were distributed evenly over the bare unfinished surface. Forsyth sat near the head of the table and poured himself a mug of black coffee. It was so hot that the pitcher steamed in the cool air of the mess hall, as Forsyth passed it to the others.

Babe filled his heavy china mug when the pitcher reached him and looked around the table for the can of condensed milk. There was a thick bowl of caked sugar in the center of the table, but there was no can of milk. Babe signaled the mess attendant who was walking between the tables.

"Where's the canned milk?" he asked.

"We done run out again, suh," the boy said. "Stewa'd says he'll try'n have some fo' tonight."

Babe reached for the sugar bowl and helped himself with an oversize spoon.

"We get what we can from the Army," Forsyth said. "Unless we get more supplies we'll be out of sugar too." He drank his black, unsweetened coffee from the chipped mug.

"I've got a friend who's a Quartermaster," one of the fliers said. "If things get worse I'll see what he can do."

"The hell with that," another said. "I don't want anything from the Dog-Faces."

"He's all right," the first flier said. "For a Doggie, he's a good guy."

Babe heard the mess boy talking to Forsyth.

"We got flapjacks an' bacon, suh," the boy said.

"Any syrup?" Forsyth asked.

"Only sorghum," the boy said.

"Any butter?"

"Jus' the regular wax, suh."

"Bring it on," Forsyth said, "warm if possible."

When the mess boy looked at him, Babe nodded. "Only one jack for me," he said. If he ate more he got bilious when he flew.

"That dry cereal last week," a flier said, "it was pretty good for a change."

"This week it's different," the second flier said. "There's no milk and no cereal to put it on." He got up from the table and wiped his mouth on the back of his arm as he took his cap from his belt and stuck it on his head. The gesture was automatic.

The mess boy came back from the galley with Babe's and Forsyth's plates. The single flapjack on Babe's plate was burned. It was thick and heavy. He dug his knife into the pale glob of wax on the plate and buttered his pancake. Forsyth passed him the syrup mug and Babe poured out thick brown sorghum. The mess boy held an aluminum dish of bacon beside him and Babe took two pieces with his fork. The bacon was half-hidden in the bottom of the dish by the dark grease. Probably cooked last night, Babe thought. He looked at the little brown bottle of atabrine in the center of the table. A mess boy filled his steel water cup and Babe reached for the salt pills. He took two in the palm of his hand and swallowed them down with a drink of water. Then he began to eat the thick gummy flapjack covered by the soursweet molasses.

One of the intelligence officers came in and sat down beside Babe. He poured himself a mug of coffee and lighted a cigarette.

" 'Morning, Dave," Forsyth said.

"Hello, Eliot."

"What's on your mind?"

The officer laughed. "Should there be something on my mind?" He popped an atabrine pill into his mouth, washing it down with coffee.

"You're Intelligence," Forsyth said. "You're supposed to be hitting on sixteen cylinders all the time. What's up?"

"Your strike was called off last night," he said, "but that wasn't the only thing on the books."

"No?" Forsyth said. "What else? Did the Army try bombing old volcanos again?"

"The Army didn't fly either," the officer said. He put down

his coffee mug. "There was a task force off Munda last night."

"What happened?" Babe asked.

"They shelled the hell out of Charlie's airstrip."

"Good," Forsyth said. "That's fine." He balanced a bit of cold bacon on the end of his fork. "What's wrong with that?"

"Nothing," the officer said. "Except that about six hundred miles away a flight of Mitsubishis is being gassed up for a try at our cruisers."

"How do you know that?" Babe asked. He put down his knife and fork.

"Never mind how. We know."

"Where are our cruisers now?"

"Heading back, Eliot," the Intelligence Officer said. "There's five of them and a few destroyers for anti-sub protection."

"What's the picture?" Forsyth asked.

"They'll be between Tulagi and Savo at about three this afternoon," the officer said, "and, if our dope is right, Charlie will try to catch them there in the narrows where they can't maneuver."

"Can the Japs be stopped?" Babe asked.

"We've intercepted Charlie before," the officer said. "I guess we'll have another chance this afternoon."

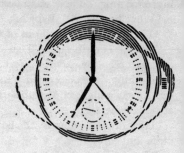

CORDELL CAME INTO THE MESS HALL FOLLOWED BY LAMBERT and walked to the table where McRae was sitting.

" 'Morning, skipper," he said. "What's the word?"

"It's the same," McRae said, passing him the coffee. "We work harder and get less food every day."

"After a while," Cordell said, "we'll be borrowing rice from Charlie."

"I'll take rice instead of this, any day," McRae said. He pushed the atabrine and the salt tablets toward Cordell.

"Powdered eggs this morning?" Cordell asked.

"No. Your favorite—collision mats and lube oil."

Cordell shook out two salt tablets and an atabrine pill. It was a grain-and-a-half pill and he halved it with his knife blade, dropping the other half back into the little brown bottle.

"How's your malaria?" McRae asked.

"Just fair," Cordell said. "I had one chill a couple of days ago."

"Tell the doc?"

"Hell, no, Larry. We were going up to Kahili that night." Cordell swallowed his pills and took a gulp of coffee. He remembered the chill hitting him in the afternoon and again at night over Santa Isabel on the way up to Bougainville. They had flown high that time and it was colder than he had expected. His body temperature had gone down from the high altitude and the chill had got him. He remembered his hands shaking on the stick and his teeth chattering so that he could not talk over the radio when McRae called him on the intercom. He reached for the molasses and began pouring it over the pancake the boy had set in front of him.

The Squadron Commander pushed aside his tin plate and lighted the pipe he always carried in his breast pocket. The others kidded him about being breasty because of the twin bulges made by the pipe and his tobacco pouch. Smoking tobacco was hard to get and he used his only a few times each day. This week he was using cigarette tobacco, separated from the paper and mixed with a few grains of an aromatic blend he had got in Auckland. He drew in deeply and blew the gray smoke over Cordell's head. He could hear the sound of planes on Henderson.

Cordell looked up from his breakfast. "What the hell are you smoking, Larry?" he asked.

McRae took the pipe from his mouth. "My own mixture. Ninety-five percent tobacco shreds from America's Finest Low-Priced Smoke and the rest a rather good New Zealand leaf."

"At breakfast," Cordell growled, "the smoking lamp should be out." Until he came to the Solomons he smoked, but he had got sick of having his cigarette packages wet through with his own sweat. When he stopped smoking he was getting only two or three cigarettes from a pack.

Most of the officers had left the mess hall. The few who were still there smoked and talked, while the mess boys cleaned off the tables and went over the bare boards with damp rags.

Forsyth got up from the table and walked over to McRae.

23

"What's the program today, sir?" he asked.

"I'm not sure yet," McRae said. "I'm going over to Strike Command in a little while and see what they've got doped out for us."

"Think we'll have a strike tonight?"

"I don't know," McRae said. "But the weather looks good enough."

"Thank God the rains are over," Cordell said. "I don't mind the heat the way I did that God-damned rain. I'm not dried out yet."

Forsyth put on his cap. "If you want me later I'll be in my tent."

"I'll let you know what they say over at Strike," Larry said. "No sense in worrying about it until we know for sure."

"Right," Forsyth said. He turned and walked down between the tables, his heavy ankle shoes pounding the rough floor boards. Babe Lewis got up from his table and followed Forsyth out of the mess hall. A mess boy cleared away his place quickly and another boy brought a new set-up.

Cordell drank from the metal cup and wiped his hands on his thighs. "That was lousy," he said. "I think I'll go over to Sick Bay and draw a K-Ration for lunch."

McRae laughed. "You're not used to good food like that, Joe. You'll get fat."

"Fat—hell," Cordell said sourly. "I'd be happy if I could get enough at mealtimes to keep something between my skin and my bones. Right now they rub together every time I move and it itches like hell."

"Well," McRae said, "maybe we'll get a Liberty ship in tomorrow."

"If we do, it'll be another six months before she's unloaded. Half the food will be rotten then and none of us will be around to eat the rest."

"You're right, Joe," McRae said soberly. "I wonder if any of us will be alive when the squadron's relieved."

"We're all trying to figure that one out," Joe said. "Each guy probably thinks he'll go back alive and all the rest will get posthumous Navy Crosses."

"It's the only way we can figure it out here," McRae said, "If we didn't think we had at least a chance of getting back to the mainland we wouldn't be worth a damn—we'd be finished before we got started." He heard Lambert walk up behind him.

"You're wrong, Larry," Lambert said. "It depends on the guy. A guy who's fighting just to get back to the States is only half-fighting. But if he thinks about the things we were sent out here to do—if he looks west toward the other islands the Japs have—then when he gets knocked off it may come as a surprise to him but it won't be a horrible disappointment."

"How many think that way?" Cordell said.

"Not many," Lambert said. "Maybe not enough."

"Do you?"

"Yes. I think I do."

"You're not married," Cordell said.

"No," Ben said very quietly in the still mess hall. "I never had a chance." He started to put on his cap and heard a P-38 whine down toward the palms. "Joe," he said, "I didn't even get a good look around."

He turned and walked toward the door, holding his cap in his hand, and the others watched him as he opened the screen door and let it slam shut behind him.

Cordell looked at McRae. "He's crazy."

"No, he's not, Joe," McRae said. "He's been slapped around a lot and seen most of his friends get killed, but he's not crazy. Ben wants to go back as much as you or I do, but first he wants to see how close he can get to Charlie's backyard." McRae got up from the bench and edged along the table to the aisle.

"Going back to your tent?" Cordell asked.

"No. Over to Strike Command. I'll let you know what cooks."

"Thanks, skipper. If I know in advance what we're going to do, it gives me time to write letters."

As they walked out into the clearing McRae looked up above the palms and saw an F4U doing snap rolls at 15,000 feet. The two of them stood there watching, while the little silver plane twisted and spun with the sun glinting from its wings three miles above Henderson.

Babe Lewis had spread his wet soapy khakis on the washing bench beside Forsyth's tent and was scrubbing the dark cotton with a borrowed ki-yi brush. He was not used to washing his own clothes and it was hard for him to hold the shirt against the top of the bench with one hand while he scrubbed up and down with the other. When he had scrubbed the back he laid out the sleeve and soaped the cuff rim. Then he scrubbed again, watching the darker line of dirt disappear. He scrubbed the other cuff and then the collar the same way. He filled a helmet with water from the can and rinsed the shirt several times, changing the water for each rinsing. Then he carried the shirt over to a wire that ran between two palms and hung it so that half the shirt was on each side of the wire, the sleeves hanging down and the collar flattened and pulled out. When the shirt dried it would be fairly presentable. He had seen Forsyth do shirts the same way.

The breeze swayed the shirt a little in the sun and Babe was sure it would be dry by noon. He went back to the helmet and stirred a pair of gray wool issue socks in the cold soapy water. He wrung them out, rinsed them and hung them on the wire beside the shirt. Then he began scrubbing a pair of khaki shorts with the ki-yi, soaping the fabric well so that it would be sure to bleach. He was working up perspiration, and when he had rinsed the shorts and hung them on the wire, he put a pair of skivvy shorts and shirt into the helmet to soak. Then he brushed the sweat from his forehead and went inside the tent.

Forsyth was lying on his cot watching the roof of the tent. "How'd it go?" he asked.

"Okay," Babe said. He took out a cigarette and sat down at the table. "I'm out of matches," he said. "Have you got any?"

"Nobody has," Forsyth said. He rolled on his side and pulled out a lighter.

"Thanks," Babe said. He inhaled deeply and handed the lighter back to Eliot.

"Where were you born, Babe?" Forsyth asked.

"Indiana."

"Want to get back?"

"Yes."

Eliot rolled over and looked at him. "Then why'd you become a torpedo pilot?"

"I don't know," Babe said. "Maybe because I was the youngest in my class at Pensacola. I wanted to show them I could do it."

"Married long?"

"Three months," Babe said. He reached into his hip pocket and brought out his wallet. "Here's her picture."

Forsyth looked at the picture. It showed a rather pretty blonde girl kneeling beside a collie dog. Her face wore a fixed smile as though she had been posing a long time. She might have been Swedish.

"Like her?" Forsyth asked.

Babe put back the wallet. "I'm crazy about her," he said

"That's why I want to get the war over—so I can go back to her and start raising children."

"A good reason," Eliot said. He lay on his back and watched the roof of the tent again.

"Do you think we'll have a strike tonight?"

"I don't know yet," Eliot said. "The skipper said he'd let me know after he came back from Strike Command."

He watched a fly buzz angrily around the apex of the tent until it flew down near the table. As he followed it with his eye he saw that Babe was sitting on his cot looking at his moldy blues while the smoke from his cigarette drifted up slowly through the still air of the tent.

Lambert was standing in front of his tent taking his dry clothes from the wire when he saw McRae drive his jeep down the road.

"Where away, Larry?" he shouted.

"Over to Strike. Want a ride?"

"Sure." Lambert took his clothes inside the tent and jogged down the sunbaked road to McRae's jeep.

"Where're you going?" McRae asked as he pushed the little car into gear.

"I'd like to hear what tonight's plans are. Anyway I need the air." He put on his colored glasses to shield his eyes from the sun and the dust. The jeep hit a rut and jostled him, making his wrist band hit the edge of the seat. They turned to the right and went up a long bumpy hill that was the crest of Henderson. From the top of it they could see the bomber strip below them—the B-17s and the Liberators, the Black Cats and the Hudsons—and in the revetment area, carefully dispersed behind mounds of rubble, sat their Avengers. They could smell the dust already and it grew thicker as they went down the other side of the hill toward the runway. They drove past groups of small tents and bomb dumps, skirting the edge of

28

the taxi apron until they were on the far side approaching a dugout in the side of the hill. There were rows of sandbags piled around the entrance and over it, between two rows, was a neatly painted sign:

STRIKE COMMAND

Lambert turned to McRae. "Whenever I see that it always makes me think it should be *Cave Canem*."

"Or—Abandon Hope," Larry said.

He stopped the jeep and pulled on the brake. The dust swirled up around them and they walked quickly from it into the entrance below the sign.

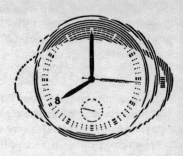

STRIKE COMMAND WAS THE COOLEST PLACE AT HENDERSON Field. Its walls were thick cement, heavily coated with whitewash, and the operations rooms had a bare cement floor. There were maps and charts tacked to the walls and on one side there was an operational blackboard. As reports came in from the control tower the duty sergeant erased some of the little boxes, changing figures or names.

McRae went over and looked at the weather chart.

Lambert saw Paul Scott at the duty officer's desk, a field phone wedged between his shoulder and ear, another phone in his left hand, and a pen in his right. He was taking down a message and Lambert waited until he had hung up the phone.

"Hello, Paul," he said. "Busy morning?"

"Christ, yes," Scott said. He laughed and Ben could see that he was tired and unshaven.

"What's up?"

"Me for one thing—all night. The call was from communications. One of the SBD boys reporting. Thinks he's spotted Barnes."

"Where?"

"A little island off New Georgia. Dropped him a message on the beach telling him to build a bonfire tonight. We'll send up a Cat after him."

"Is he all right?"

"Don't know yet. How long's he been missing?"

"Five weeks," Lambert said. He remembered the night Barnes had not returned from Vila.

"They've come back okay after longer than that," Scott said. The phone on his shoulder began to crackle. He listened to the voice for a while. "Roger," he said, and rang off.

"Had breakfast?" Ben asked.

"Not yet, Ben. All I want is coffee."

"If you're sending up a Cat tonight, the weather must look good."

"It does." McRae was behind them.

"How about the strike?"

"I'm going up to see the Commander now." He went out of the room to the interior ladder that led up to the briefing shack on the hilltop.

"Hear the dope, Ben?" Scott asked.

"About this afternoon?"

"Yeah. Charlie's coming over. . . . 'In force' as the communiqués say."

"Scared?"

"Not in this fur-lined foxhole. I welcome Condition Red just for the chance to crawl back to our luxurious air-conditioning."

"I don't think you ever leave," Lambert said. "Hell, I'd bring my sack here if I were you."

"Next week," Scott said. "I'm working up to it." He yawned and shook his head, his eyes beginning to water.

"Come on over for a drink this evening."

"Thanks. I'd like to. Going to the flick?"

"What is it?"

"*The Gold Rush,* I think."

"I've seen it before."

"I've seen them all before. Most of the ones we get here I've seen two or three times. I must have seen every flick made in 1940."

"What'd the cruisers do last night?"

"A good job, they tell me," Scott said. "Al Thomas went up with the spotting crews. Says they threw a hell of a lot of stuff on the strip. From up there it looked colorful as hell."

"Has the mail plane come in yet?"

"Don't think so, Ben. About an hour."

A Marine corporal came in with a cup of coffee for Scott.

"Have some, Ben?"

"No, thanks. I may fly a little later."

"Our coffee's good here—mild as a Manhattan." Scott took a sip and leaned back in his chair. "Christ," he said, "I wish my relief would come." The phone rang and he picked it up. "Strike Command," he said.

When he had rung off he looked at Lambert, who was sitting on a bomb crate seat. "The SBDs are coming back," he said.

"All of them?"

"Don't know yet. Let's count them when they come in."

Lambert took a package of cigarettes from his breast pocket. The paper was wet already. "Want one, Paul?"

"Got a dry one?"

"I'll feel." He fingered around the inside of the package, brought out two fairly dry cigarettes and gave one to Scott.

"There's a plane now," Scott said, listening. "Let's watch them come in. I need a breath of air." He got up from the table and his .45 holster caught awkwardly on the arm of his chair until he twisted free.

"Take it easy, soldier," Lambert said. He followed Scott

out of the entrance between the rows of sandbags and put on his dark glasses as the sun hit him. He pulled down the visor of his baseball cap and looked at the east end of the field.

"Bad guess," he said to Scott. "That's a Hudson coming in."

They stood side by side on the hill, feeling the sea wind on their bare legs and the sun on their shoulders while the New Zealander's Hudson banked into the wind as it lost altitude in its approach.

Lambert saw the sun reflect from the blue-white camouflage of the plane and then he grabbed Scott's arm. "Look, Paul," he said. "It's in trouble."

Scott heard the pilot trying to gun the engines again and then he saw that the landing gear was not yet down. The plane came lower and lower and finally the nose went up a little as it glided a few feet over the runway, its flaps dropping like a gull's feathers. They watched the plane drop closer to the surface of Henderson, and now that there were palms in the background they could see how fast she was going. Then suddenly a little plume of dust rose up where the tail dragged the ground, widening as the fuselage came parallel to the runway, and as her belly struck, a billow of dust came up around the plane, and they could see it jerk back and forth. The tearing sound of the breaking body came to them through the quiet air and then the staccato thuds of the propellers beating against the earth as she skidded along, slowing perceptibly, one wing down, until she came to rest half-way down the strip and the dust of Henderson came up around her in a brown whirling cloud that rose high above her and hid her until the wind dissipated it. They could see the Hudson lying brokenly on the strip with the ambulance pulling up to her and men running toward her.

"Easy, boy," Ben said, when Scott started down the hill toward the Hudson.

"I'm going down," he said. "They might be hurt."

"Maybe they are. What could you do?"

Scott stopped and looked at Lambert. "I don't know," he said. "I just thought I ought to go down."

"Look now," Lambert said. "There's nothing we can do."

Scott turned and saw the crowd of men standing around the smashed plane. An ambulance was alongside and he could see the doors open as the Corpsmen took out the stretchers. He walked back up the hill toward Lambert.

"Of course," he said. "Don't know why I wanted to tear down. Only be in the way."

"Natural enough," Ben said. "You haven't seen many crack-ups, have you?"

"Only a few. Have you?"

"Yes. Always the guys sitting next to me or flying beside me, but never me."

"You've got a lot of luck."

"I wonder," Ben said slowly. "Maybe it's not time yet."

Down by the plane they could see two men on stretchers being put into the rear of the ambulance. Three New Zealanders from the plane stood at the end of the ambulance watching while the doors were closed. Then the ambulance scurried off across the runway, its spinning wheels throwing up a veil of dust.

A Marine private hurried up the hill to them.

"What happened?" Scott asked.

"Navigator says ack-ack knocked out the hydraulic system."

"Where the hell did the ack-ack come from?"

"Rekata Bay, sir. They dropped a few bombs on the way back."

"Damn fools," Scott said. "They had orders to stay away from there."

"Maybe they got tired of sending in weather reports," Lambert said. "Those recco and weather missions are hell after a few months. Why don't you give them some action?"

"They haven't got the planes," Scott said.

"Get some from the Army," Lambert said. "Those New Zealanders can fly."

"I don't make the decisions, Ben. You know that."

"They ought to get a break. That's all they live for."

"Does it make that much difference to them?"

"Yes. They do a good job on weather and reconnaissance and dropping flares for us to get back at night, hoping there'll be a shift for them some day. But the guys who sit back here in their Quonset huts figure they're so good they won't change them."

"Maybe they're right," Scott said.

"No, they aren't. Men get stale after a while. They'll do anything for a change. That's why the N-Zedders took a chance over Rekata this morning."

"Couldn't they have flown over by mistake?"

"No," Ben said. "They're the best navigators in the world. After you've flown up the Slot a few times it's impossible to get lost in daylight. If anything crazy ever happens to me it'll be because I got sick of mining and plunge-bombing and torpedoing supply barges."

"What more do you want?"

"I'd like to check out in a fighter."

"Will you?"

"No. I'm too valuable as a torpedo pilot. We're harder to replace."

Some mechs had gathered around the Hudson and were hooking the fuselage to a tow truck.

"Can they fix up that plane?" Scott asked.

"At Henderson," Ben said, "they can do anything."

He saw a little silver line in the sky over Koli Point and heard the flat drone of the first SBD's engine.

"There they are," Scott said. He shaded his eyes, watching the Dauntless jockey for a cross-wind landing. There were three of them visible and the roar of their engines grew louder as they came in.

The tow truck was pulling the Hudson toward the far side of the runway, clear of the planes that were about to land. The first Dauntless, its flaps down, skimmed stiff-legged over the landing strip and its nose went up a little as it stalled in.

"One," Scott counted.

"How many were there?"

"Ten."

"Two," Lambert said. The first plane was at the far end of Henderson and he could see the puff of dust as the pilot kicked the brakes.

"Three," Scott said. They counted silently until eight had landed.

"There's Nine," Ben said. The plane limped in over the edge of the strip, its engine coughing badly. The pilot pancaked her in, and she bounced high, taking the full shock on her landing struts. The engine died and she mushed down the runway, little spurts of dust rising as she skipped along, and slowed when the pilot touched the brakes.

"Where's Ten?" Scott said.

"Where do you think?"

"Maybe he'll come in later."

"Don't be a fool, Paul. If he comes back it'll be in a rubber boat. Ten went out and only nine got back. That's a pretty good average I'd say. For our Avengers, it's unheard of."

"I know it, Ben. I don't like to think about it, I guess."

"Why not?" Lambert said slowly. "I think about it all the time. It's not much fun to eat at mess with the boys and look around you and wonder who won't be there tomorrow morning."

"No," Scott said, "it isn't."

"Then face it, Paul. Pilots are just part of planes, and out here they're easier to replace. If we lost a plane, a pilot and a gunner over Munda this morning, perhaps we killed a hundred Nips and knocked out a dozen Zeros. You can't complain against odds like that."

"I guess not." Scott heard someone walk up behind him and turned to see his relief saluting.

"Ready to relieve you, sir," the officer said.

"She's all yours," Paul said. "The SBD pilots will be here in a minute or so."

"Anything else?"

"Don't think so. We may have lost one pilot this morning."

"Say 'plane'," Lambert said. "That's what's important."

"Very well," the officer said. "I relieve you, sir."

"Thanks," Scott said, saluting back.

A truck rumbled around the bottom of the hill and Lambert could see it was the dive-bomber crews coming up for questioning.

"Is the Commander still here?" Lambert asked.

"Probably up there with your skipper."

"Are you going to sit in on the post-mortem?"

"No," Scott said. "I'm going back to my tent for some sleep."

"Don't forget to come over tonight."

"I'll be there." Scott walked down into the operations room, his .45 holster slapping his thigh.

Lambert folded his arms and watched the SBD pilots jump out of the lorry and walk up the hill to the briefing room. Some wore helmets on the back of their heads, but most of them had on wool baseball caps and dark glasses. Their khakis were bleached and greasy; their short-sleeved shirts grayed and torn, but they walked with an air and a swagger, feeling the weight of their .45s and their sheath knives on their hips—their Mae Wests over their shoulders, their tan leather gloves in their hands—the bloody, sunburned wonders of Henderson.

They climbed up beside him and he watched them go, talking or laughing or silent, and he could see their unshaved chins and the darkness under their eyes as they went up the last few yards to the shack at the top of the hill.

He watched the last one go into the screened veranda and saw McRae edge his way out. The skipper had a sheaf of papers in his hands and he waved them at Lambert as he strode down the hillside toward him.

"Got the dope?" Ben asked.

"I sure have, lad," McRae said, smiling.

"What have they got for us?"

"Kahili tonight," McRae said. "A hell of a big strike."

They walked down to the jeep together and Lambert tasted the dryness of his mouth.

"Do we all go?"

"Yes," McRae said. "Every TBF we can get into the air." He backed the jeep down to the taxi apron and Lambert held on to the metal seat while they bounced over the mat toward the Squadron.

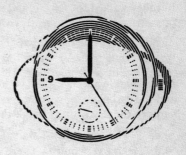

*B*ABE WATCHED FORSYTH TAKE A PAIR OF MARINE SHOES FROM his sea chest and start to scrape mud from the rough leather with the dull edge of his sheath knife. The mud had been there for a long time and it came off in cakes. When he had finished the upper, Forsyth started scraping along the sole. Little triangles of mud fell to the floor between his feet.

"What's there to do this morning?" Babe asked.

"Same as any other morning," Forsyth said, without looking up. "Nothing. You haven't been here very long. Are you bored already?"

"God, yes," Babe said.

"Some of us run out of things to do before the rest," Forsyth said. "I brought a crossword-puzzle book with me and it lasted almost four days."

"What'd you do then?"

"Climbed Kokumbona for souvenirs; tried surf fishing; reread all the old magazines; drank coffee all day and, finally, when all that was no good, I started remembering."

"Remembering what?"

"The days of my youth."

"Did that help?"

"For a while," Forsyth said. "Then even the most perfect memories became hackneyed and a little ludicrous and I got to the point where it seemed as though I'd never done anything worth remembering." He put down the finished shoe and picked up the other.

"Did getting mail help any?"

"Not much," Forsyth said. He began scraping the second shoe. "The one letter I waited for never came, so the rest didn't count very much. There must be a lot of guys who go through life waiting for a letter they'll never get."

"I'd like to get one from my wife today."

"That's not quite what I mean," Eliot said. "I'm enough of a romanticist to think that nothing's ever really finished. You can't stop being in love with a girl just because she married another guy."

"Is that what's wrong?"

"Yes," Forsyth said. He stopped scraping the shoe. "It doesn't make any difference to me if it's hot or rainy or if I'm here or in Frisco, or if I fly on the strikes or sit here in this tent. The only thing that matters is that a girl with the darkest eyes in the world married a guy who's a jerk."

"After you were in the Navy?"

"No. Before. Maybe that's one reason I went in."

"Is she in love with you now?"

"Perhaps," Forsyth said slowly. "Yes, very likely she is."

"But she's married," Babe said. He did not like the idea of anybody being in love with somebody else's wife.

"Sometimes, Babe, being in love doesn't mean getting married—nor getting married, being in love."

"Why would anybody get married if they weren't in love?"

"Lots of reasons," Forsyth said. "Some of them aren't very

pretty—like getting a lien on a guy's bankbook or his ancestral acres."

"Is that what she did?" Babe asked.

"Yes," Forsyth said. "That's what happened."

"I knew Marge all my life," Babe said. "I never went with any other girls."

"That's the way it ought to be," Forsyth said, "but sometimes it doesn't happen like that."

"Did you know a lot of girls?"

"I suppose so," Forsyth said, "but in the East so many of them were alike that I feel safer in saying I knew several different types."

The waspish whine of a Wildcat diving above them came through the walls of the tent.

"Sounds like a steep one," Forsyth said.

"Yeah," said Babe. "I hope he pulls out all right."

They listened for a moment until the pitch of the sound dropped. The plane had leveled off and was flying away.

"I wanted to be a lawyer," Eliot said. "Instead, I fly a big pregnant plane that spawns at night. She didn't want to marry and live with me while I went through law school. I wanted a couple of letters after my name in gold leaf—a decent career that could support us and give our kids a chance."

"What happened?"

"I stopped kidding myself and admitted that the war was bound to come. She didn't believe me. Anyway, Harvard gave me back my first semester's deposit. Within two months she was engaged to a guy she met at a party and I went down to Pensacola. I didn't even get an announcement."

"That sounds pretty raw."

"She must have been afraid I'd show up at the wedding, but there wasn't much chance of that. You know how much leave you got at Pensacola."

41

"Damn little," Babe said.

"It makes quite a story," Forsyth said. "I always like to tell it when I get a few drinks in me. Maybe this evening."

"I'd like to hear it," Babe said. He wondered if it was true that a lot of guys waited for a letter that never came.

Cordell drove over the road toward the revetment area. He had forgotten his colored glasses and now that the trucks had been over the road, the hard surface was ground into fine flour that was stirred up by the jeep's front wheels and blown over the hood into his face. He slowed a little and the dust receded. Some day when he got a chance he would take the jeep down to the motor pool and get a windshield for it. A bomb had blown out the pane months ago and he had never got around to getting another. He heard a truck rumbling up behind and he pulled over to the side of the road. The truck passed, throwing a high thick screen of dust over the roadside, covering the jeep with a layer of brown powder as it went by. Cordell closed his eyes and waited until the truck was a hundred yards ahead. He coughed as he opened his eyes and saw the truck ahead doling out dust the way a sprinkler scatters water. He felt for his canteen and swallowed a few gulps of water. It cleared his throat and he headed the jeep back on the road again. A cross path led across the main road, and, turning down it, he saw the Avengers standing like mastiffs chained to their rubble kennels.

Cordell drove over the link mat to his plane. Wazinski, the plane captain was inside the cockpit, and he could see his tail gunner loading a .30 belt into a drum. Cordell turned off the ignition and hopped out of the jeep.

" 'Morning, sir," the gunner said.

The plane captain looked out of the cockpit. " 'Morning, Mr. Cordell," he said, touching his cap.

"Hello," Cordell said, wiping the dust from his forehead. He took off his cap and shook the dust from it. "How's the plane?"

"Ready any time," Ski said. "I'm just checking the bomb bays."

"Could you stop that oil leak?"

"Yes, sir. No trouble at all. I took your chute over to the loft for repacking. They'll have it ready this afternoon."

"That's soon enough," Cordell said. "I won't be flying this morning."

"Are we flying tonight, sir?" the gunner asked.

"Yes," Cordell said. "There's a strike tonight. Don't let the word get around, though."

"No, sir," the gunner said.

"Check all the guns, will you?" Cordell said, "and tell Sparks to take a look at the radio some time this afternoon. I don't want any trouble with the damn thing tonight."

"I'll give everything a final check myself," Ski said. "Any chance of going along?"

"Afraid not," Cordell said, squinting up at the sun. "We'll have a hell of a bomb load."

"When shall I bomb-up, sir?"

"I'll let you know after Strike Briefing this afternoon. It'll either be mines or a big baby."

"Right, sir. I'll have the ordnance man get ready for one or the other."

Cordell walked around the tail of the big TBF. The elevator surfaces had three cloth patches that were not yet painted. Tracers had caught him there on the last strike. He moved his hand lightly over the aluminum skin of the fuselage, feeling the little heat blisters that were raised on the silver-blue camouflage paint.

"Let's get her painted soon," Cordell said.

"There's not much paint," Ski said, "but I'll see what I can get. I guess they've stopped sending us supplies."

"There'll be some along any day," Cordell said, but he knew that other things would come before paint.

"When are we going to be relieved, sir?" the gunner asked.

"Next week," Cordell said, "or next month, or next year."

"They can't keep us out here forever, can they?"

"Yes," Cordell said. "Why not? Maybe there's nobody else to do the job."

"There's another squadron in Fiji . . ."

"They're training," Cordell said. "Practicing night landings and learning something about plunge-bombing. They didn't get much of that at Alameda."

"They might be getting ready to take our place, sir."

"Maybe," Cordell said. "Or perhaps they'll be coming over to fly with us. It wouldn't hurt to have a few more of us on a strike."

"I bet a guy ten bucks we were going to be relieved in two weeks."

"Save your money," Cordell said, "and next time don't bet." He bent down under the wing and looked at the folded bomb bays streaked with dust and oil. Then he walked forward and turned so that he could see the chipped leading edge of the wing. He rubbed the lower blade of the propeller with one hand and felt its deepening pits—as though it had been sand-blasted. The paint had worn off long ago and the blade edges had become roughened. Some day when Ski had time, he would have him pull the prop and check its balance.

He heard a jeep driving up to the next revetment and saw that it was McRae. The skipper got out and his plane captain appeared from under the wing. McRae was carrying his helmet and his Mae West. Cordell got in his jeep and drove over to McRae's revetment.

"Where to, Larry?"

"Over to Russell and back, Joe." He began to put on his helmet. "Want a ride?"

"Not now. I'm going to take it easy until after lunch. If you see anybody I know over there, give 'em my regards."

"Glad to. I'll be back in about an hour."

"See you at mess."

"Right." McRae ducked under the wing and climbed up on the step below the cockpit. He pulled the cowling panel back and got into the cockpit. He could hear the plane captain walking inside by the radio aft. He plugged on his phones and switched the selector to inter-com.

He pressed the speaker button of his phone. "Hello, Thompson," he said. "What's the word?"

"All set, sir," his earphones answered.

McRae switched to Liaison. *"Knucklehead to Tower,"* he said. *"Knucklehead to Tower; come in; come in."*

There was a moment before the Control Officer answered: *"Tower to Knucklehead; Tower to Knucklehead. I am receiving you. Modulation good. Runway clear shortly. Runway clear shortly."*

"Roger," McRae said. "Roger." He checked and saw that his wheels were locked, bomb bays closed, flaps down. He switched on the ignition, moved the throttle ahead, changed the mixture to Rich, and the gas to Auxiliary Tank. He waggled the stick and rudder pedals.

Cordell heard the starter cartridge explode and saw the long flames lick back under the engine vents as the prop spun, reflecting the sunlight like glass. The exhaust flames receded as McRae changed the mixture and the engine revved as he pushed the throttle ahead. Cordell got into his jeep, watching the big Grumman shudder as the engine warmed. Then McRae released the brakes and the plane inched ahead, slowly at first, onto the metal taxi strip and then, as it moved faster, the dust whirled up behind it and Cordell turned away until the plane was farther down the mat, rumbling and bumping along toward the end of the strip.

McRae turned the plane so that it faced the length of the runway and put on the brakes. He pressed the phone button. *"Knucklehead to Tower; Knucklehead to Tower—permission to take off. Permission to take off."* He put down the phone and looked on either side of the plane. The runway was clear.

"Tower to Knucklehead; Tower to Knucklehead—you may take off now. You may take off now."

McRae shoved the throttle ahead and the plane vibrated as though it would tear itself loose in spite of the brakes. He slid the plastic cowling ahead and locked it. Then he centered the stick and the rudder pedals. He released the brakes and the Avenger moved jerkily ahead over the uneven mat, bouncing from side to side as its speed increased and then the tail had lifted a little and he moved the stick forward. The tail came up and, with the throttle full, the plane passed the Control Tower. McRae could feel it bounce easily as the wings began to take the weight. It would have flown itself off if he had not pulled the stick back a bit and brought up the nose. He felt the wheels leave the ground, and the vibration of their spinning continued as he moved the hydraulic lever to retract them. The drag of the plane decreased and now he was over the end of Henderson and the palms fifty feet below. He banked lightly to the left and came back over the revetment area. Below him he could see Cordell's jeep bumping down the cross-path to the road and he banked again and headed out over the palms toward Russell Island.

At four hundred feet he slipped into his seat pack and snapped his safety belt. The green of Guadalcanal changed abruptly to the white of Lunga Beach and then to the light greens and blues of the shoal water. Off Lunga Point, where the water was deeper, some Liberty ships were being unloaded by amphibious trucks. They looked like water bugs skittering from the ships toward land, and then he was over them and headed toward Savo. He climbed to 3,000 feet and the top of Savo seemed next to his cockpit. Levelling off, he eased the mixture to Lean and heard the engine settle back to a medium-pitched drone that purred powerfully in his ears.

The sun was behind him, and, as he looked down, he could see it silvering the bright surface of Iron Bottom Bay, where the cruisers had got it that night. To the left, beached on Esperance, were the Jap transports that the dive bombers had caught. They were rusted and gutted, and he could see the dark flame-scarred hulks that had meant the Japs' last chance at the Solomons. The next time he was sent a bunch of kid torpedo-pilots, he'd work up a plunge-bombing schedule for them, using the transports as targets.

McRae saw the compass swing a little and he brought the plane back on its course as he headed up the Slot toward the air strip at Russell.

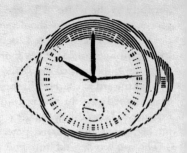

$\mathcal{L}$AMBERT AND FORSYTH DROVE OUT OF THE SQUADRON AREA-way toward Henderson. Lambert was driving and he took a shortcut through the crews' area. He was watching the deep, hard ruts in the road and trying to dodge them when he felt Forsyth's hand on his shoulder.

"Look, Ben," Forsyth said. He pointed to three young Marines standing in front of a tent.

Lambert slowed and looked at them. The two youngest were posing together while the third tried to catch them in the viewfinder of his camera. Ben saw that they were holding a skull between them, decorated with a flier's baseball cap and colored glasses. The two young Marines squinted happily at the morning sunlight and the glasses gleamed brilliantly for a moment as the sun struck them.

"What's that dangling there?"

Forsyth strained his eyes. "It's a necklace of some kind, Ben. Maybe teeth."

"Yeah," Lambert said. "That'd be it. Teeth." He stepped on the accelerator and they moved around behind some palms that cut the three Marines from view.

"You'd think it was a basketball trophy," Forsyth said as the jeep bumped along.

"How old do you suppose they are?"

"Seventeen—eighteen, maybe."

"They don't look old enough to be out here."

"Kids have new games now," Forsyth said.

"And new toys."

They came into a clearing beside Henderson and, looking up at the faint sound of an approaching plane, saw a C-47 cargo plane coming in over Koli Point.

"That could be the mail plane," Forsyth said.

"I'll get out at Scat Operations," Lambert said. "If there's any mail for the Squadron, I'll bring it back."

"No," Forsyth said. "Easier for me to get a ride back from the revetments. Take me there and keep the jeep."

Lambert drove onto the taxi mat and let Forsyth out beside his plane. "Any bets on the mail, Eliot?"

"Sure," Forsyth grinned. "Neither you or I will get any."

"At least I write," Lambert said. "You never do."

"Everybody's married," Forsyth said. "They're too busy to answer."

Lambert turned the jeep around and headed down the edge of Henderson to the Southern Combat Air Transport Operations tent. He pulled up in front of it and watched the converted commercial plane land. It had been sprayed a dull brown and, as far away as he was, he could see where the paint had been worn from the wings and the stabilizer and near the big cargo door. The plane landed easily and stopped near the end of the field. It skidded around with a roar as the pilot headed her back along the edge of the runway.

Some mechs and the duty officer got in a jeep and drove out to meet the plane. When the engines stopped, the dust died down and the cargo door was swung open. Lambert started his jeep again and drove slowly out on the field, stopping about fifty feet from the plane. The pilot and co-pilot jumped out and then the radioman. Lambert tried to look inside the fuselage to see if the piles of mail sacks were there, but a figure in an Army flight jacket, with a long-brimmed hat, jumped down to the ground. Ben watched it curiously until he realized suddenly that it was an Army nurse. He noticed the roundness of her body and then, as she turned toward him in the sunlight, he saw it was Ann Robinson.

Lambert pushed back his cap and stood up in the jeep. "Hello, Ann," he said. "How was the trip?"

She ran over to him, her heavy Army shoes scuffing the dirt of the runway. "Ben," she said breathlessly, "I'm so glad you're here." She took off her cap and her long brown hair fell down around her shoulders. "It's been so long since Sydney."

"And Honolulu," Ben said.

"Honolulu's like a lost world," Ann said. She stood beside the jeep fumbling with the brim of her flying cap. "I wish I'd known you were here, Ben."

"I've been here ever since I left Australia," he said. "Where did you think I was?"

"I couldn't know," she said, "and I was afraid to ask. I knew the kind of things your squadron's been doing and I was scared to death. Oh, Ben, I wish you were safe in Noumea or Fiji or back at Pensacola, instructing."

"Well," he said, "I wanted wings. How long will you be here?"

"About half an hour," she said. "We're evacuating some of the old casualties and the plane won't be ready for a while. Is there any place we can be alone until I have to go?"

"Yes," he said. "Get in. We'll find a place." He started

the jeep and she got in beside him. He turned it around and started up the road toward the Tenaru.

"I've never been this far from Henderson before," she said.

"I hope we'll both be a lot farther away some day," he said. He looked at her and saw how lovely she was with the neck of her jacket open and her hair blowing in the wind. She turned a little and saw that he was watching her. They drove up to the top of a hill overlooking Henderson and he pulled over to the side of the road. Ben turned off the ignition and pulled her to him. His lips found the cool smoothness of her temple. She pulled off his cap and ran her fingers through his short black hair.

"Ben, darling," she said softly. "When will it be over? I'm so terribly tired."

"I don't know, Ann. Never maybe."

"Where does that leave us?"

"Where it's always leaving us—a year apart and a moment together."

"Why won't you write?" she asked slowly.

He looked away, over the field, to the green palms on the other side. "Maybe I'm thinking of you," he said. "What if the letters stopped?"

"I couldn't bear it, darling. I couldn't . . . But I keep thinking about you and wondering if you're still alive and if I'll ever see you again."

"Look, darling," he said quietly, "don't wonder about me if you can help it. Wherever I am, I'm doing the thing I wanted most. It's very simple. You don't worry about what might happen to you—don't worry about me."

"But I can't help it," she said. "It's different with you."

"No, it isn't," he said lightly. "You could crack-up in one of those flying box-cars of yours. I'm safer because I'm my own pilot."

"You can't joke me out of it, either," she said. "Oh, Ben, if it would only stop." She put her face into the hollow of his shoulder.

"No," he said. "If it stopped today it wouldn't do any good. We haven't killed enough of them yet or burned their cities or bombed them to hell the way we must. When I put away my wings I want it to be for good—not for just a few years."

"But you've done your part, Ben. You and the others have done more than men have ever been asked to do before."

"This time there's more to be done, Ann. Don't you see? We're good at our job. If we weren't doing it, it might not be done so well."

"You've done so much already. Don't you ever feel afraid or tired or sick of it, or want to stop?"

"Of course," he said. "But we've only done a little, and when we get sick of things, all we have to do is remember that morning on Ford Island and the way it was in the afternoon at Midway, and the guys in the squadron who didn't come back."

"I knew," she said. "Of course I knew. It would have to be that way with you."

"Yes," he said. "That's how it is. It's very simple."

"When will you get leave?" she asked abruptly, looking away from him.

"I'm not sure. Maybe after this operation's finished."

"When will that be?"

"Tonight's supposed to be the last time. It's a special job we've been doing for Bull Halsey."

"Are you sure it's the last night?"

"No," he said. "I'm not sure of anything. Maybe there'll be something else for next week."

"That's the trouble," she said bitterly. "There's always something else and never any end to it and never any certainty of anything at all." She put her arms around his shoulders. "I don't want anything to happen to you, Ben, and yet I know the longer you do these things, the fewer your chances are of coming out alive."

"It's the same for everybody," he said irritably. "Don't be melodramatic over it. It's no worse for me not to come back than for anybody else. Another guy might have a wife or a kid or somebody who loved him."

"Yes," she said. "Responsibilities."

"Yes," he said. "If you put it that way."

"*I've* loved you, Ben," she said, softly, and kissed his sun-burned lips.

"Forgive me," he said, simply. "I'm sorry. I've never wanted to hurt you."

"I'm glad," she said. "And I don't want you to die. Isn't that a good reason for your coming back?"

"Sure," he said, kissing her. "Sure it is."

"When you get leave I'll be in Auckland. Would you like to go to Sydney again?" She wiped some of the dust from his forehead.

"Yes," he said. "I'd like to go there. Can you get a furlough?"

"I'll try to get a week," she said. "I'm sure I can."

"Sounds fine," he said. "The first evening at Prince's . . ."

"All of our evenings will be wonderful," she said, happily, "And you won't have to take me any place unless you want to. Just being with you and knowing you're happy and safe for a while will be wonderful."

He looked at her curiously. "Do you love me that much?"

"Yes, Ben," she said. "And even if you don't love me it's all right. After all, I can't have everything, darling."

"Perhaps none of us can," he said evenly. "I wish I'd known you a long time ago."

"Before Jean?"

"Yes," he said. "It would have been perfect if I'd never known her."

"You still love her, don't you, Ben?"

"I suppose so," he said. "If a thing's real, I guess it never quite ends."

"I hoped you might hate her by now."

"No," he said. "It's easier just to forget."

They sat for a long time without saying anything, feeling the light wind from the sea and hearing the distant noises of Henderson. He held her hands and she tilted her chin to be kissed, without opening her eyes.

"Ann," he said, after a while, "what's your life like now?"

"All right, I guess," she said. "But it's always the same thing and feeling the same way and never knowing what tomorrow will be. After I go away from here this morning I'll stay a few days with a Mobile Hospital Unit, getting the patients taken care of. Then I may go to Espiritu Santo or Noumea or Nandi or Suva."

"Or Funafuti or Toṅgatabu," he grinned.

"Yes," she said. "Maybe even there. But there's never any getting away from it or hiding from the war or forgetting I'm a second lieutenant under orders."

"I know," he said. "I've felt that way, too."

"I never thought you might feel like that, Ben."

"Maybe I do right now, but it doesn't help much just to talk about it."

"It helps me," she said. "I feel better now that you know."

"Then whenever you feel that way, tell me. Don't tell anyone else, and if I'm not there, write me. I'll want to know."

"But you won't answer."

"I'll get your letters," he said. "Don't forget that."

I won't, darling," she said quietly. "I'll never forget."

She moved her arm, and her wrist fell against the steering wheel. Her wrist watch clicked against the painted metal.

"What time is it?" he asked.

"Ten forty-five," she said. "I guess we ought to go back."

"It's not very far."

"I have to make sure that all the patients are okay before we take off," she said. "That takes a few minutes."

Lambert started the jeep.

"Wait," she said. "Just let me look at you for a moment so that I can remember you the way you are now."

Ben turned toward her and she took his tanned face between her hands and kissed him. "That's all," she said. "Now we can go back."

Lambert backed the jeep around and started down the hill for Henderson.

When they drove out on the field, they could see ambulances beside the plane. Hospital Corpsmen were carrying the stretchers inside. Lambert stopped the jeep near one of the ambulances.

"Back to work now," she said. "This won't be much fun for you."

Her little laugh made his heart catch in his throat and he watched her tuck up her hair and put on the dusty khaki cap. He knew that he would always remember her that way and that for him she could never be more beautiful. She turned and ran over to the side of the plane and one of the men handed her a manifest of the patients. He saw her frown a little as she looked at the long list. Then, as she looked over at him and waved, he saw her lips form unspoken words. He waved back at her as she stepped onto the ladder and disappeared inside the dark cabin of the plane.

Ben watched the Corpsmen load the last of the stretchers aboard and once he saw her hands as she helped a stretcher aboard and then some men closed the big cargo door and the ambulances drove off.

He backed the jeep over to the edge of the field and then he heard the first engine start. The propeller swung spasmodically for an instant until the engine caught and then it spun, flashing in the sunlight while the other engine coughed into life.

The drone of the big plane increased and the dust rolled out behind it in big tan clouds as it turned and started to trundle down the edge of Henderson to the end of the runway. He started to follow the plane along, but the dust was too much and he waited there by the palms until the plane had turned again and was waiting to take off. It moved forward, gaining speed until the tail was off the ground and he wondered if she were looking for him, trying to see him somewhere along the runway that flashed by as the plane accelerated.

It lifted easily from the ground and the dust of Henderson trailed out behind it, dropping away as its wheels folded and it gained altitude before banking out over the sea. He sat there for a long time watching it until it turned into the sun and he had to look away.

After a while he turned the jeep around and headed back toward the revetment area.

He saw Forsyth standing by his plane, his hands on his hips, looking expectantly at him.

"Hello there," Eliot said.

"Hi," Ben said, driving up to him.

"Any mail?" he asked.

"Mail?" Lambert said. "What mail?"

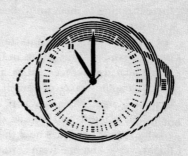

*B*ABE SAT AT THE TABLE IN THE TENT LOOKING THROUGH
a movie magazine. He never read the stories about the stars
and their lives in Hollywood; the pictures were enough for
him. He finished the magazine and threw it over in the corner where some other magazines covered a hole in the floor-
ing. Since Forsyth put the magazines over the hole, the rats
were not as noisy as they had been his first night on Guadalcanal. He had gone to the Cocoanut Bowl for movies, but
the projector had broken down and after a while they had all
left and gone back to their tents. Then somebody had
pounded on the big brass shell case that hung outside the
squadron mess and it was Condition Red. All the lights went
out, and as he ran to the slit trench he saw the searchlights
roving the sky, waiting for Charlie to fly into them. Charlie
had dropped a stick near the squadron that night and stirred
up all the rats. When the bombers had gone away he went
back to the tent and tried to sleep, but the rats had gone crazy
from the noise and the shaking of the ground and they ran
over the floor of the tent and scuffled and fought among themselves and ran across the mosquito netting, and he had lain

57

there listening to them until they quieted down and he could fall asleep.

He lighted a cigarette and stared out of the screen door at the gray trunks of the palms near by. Until he went to California he had never seen palms and when he was there he had a lot of snapshots taken of himself leaning against them to send back to Marge. Now he was sick of palms. His wrist-watch strap felt clammy and he saw that the buckle was turning green. After he got to know the mechs better, one of them might weave him one from cord or cut one from Zero aluminum. All of the other fliers seemed to have them.

Babe heard somebody walking through the soft grass toward the tent. A man looked in through the screen door.

"Lieutenant Forsyth here?"

"No, sir," Babe said. Almost everybody outranked him.

"When'll he be back?"

"Pretty soon, I guess. Want to wait?"

"Don't care if I do," the man said. He opened the door and came in. "I'm a war correspondent," he said. "I want to find out about Forsyth sinking that ship the other night." He sat down on Forsyth's bunk. "Nice place you got here," he said. "The Army don't treat me so good."

"He'd probably like to tell you himself," Babe said. "What paper do you work for?"

"One of the Washington papers," the man said. "My name's O'Bannon."

"Lewis," Babe said. They shook hands neutrally.

O'Bannon took out a dog-eared blue notebook and a short pencil. "About the ship," he said. "Did you see Forsyth do it?"

"Yes," Babe said.

"What happened?"

58

Babe felt uncomfortable. "Look," he said, "Eliot'll be here in a minute or so. He'll tell you what happened."

"How about his background, then? You know, strictly for home-town readers."

"He comes from Connecticut," Babe said. "Stamford, I think."

"Good," O'Bannon said. *"This Connecticut Yankee, scion of an Old New England family . . ."*

Babe watched the man as he wrote in the notebook. He was unhealthily fat and his jowls were pasty.

"Know anything else about him?"

"Not much," Babe said. "I haven't been here long."

"I could use a drink," the man said. "Have you got one here?"

"No," Babe said. "It's pretty hard to get, you know."

"I could pay for it," the man said. "How much? You fliers can get it easy."

"If we had any, I'd give you a drink," Babe said. "Somebody brings in a bottle once in a while, but it's for the Squadron."

"Well," the man said, "I guess I'll have to get to know you boys better. The Army gave me a jeep, but if you boys got hard stuff I might move in on you."

Babe did not say anything. He watched the man put on a pair of thick glasses.

"How about poker?" O'Bannon asked. "High stakes over here?"

"I don't know," Babe said. "I haven't played yet."

"How's your chow?"

"Not very good. The same everywhere, isn't it?"

O'Bannon groaned. "Mother of Mary, yes. I never ate so bad in my life."

"What'd you expect?" Babe asked.

59

"Three meals a day," O'Bannon said. His jowls moved when he turned his head. "Not half a meal and two bad starts."

Babe wished that Forsyth would come.

"How often do you go on strikes?"

"Whenever there's a job to do," Babe said. "Whenever the weather lets us."

"What kind of jobs have you been doing?"

"Mining Buin Harbor, torpedoing shipping, bombing their searchlights and ack-ack."

"What's this plunge-bombing like?"

"It's good," Babe said. "If that's what you want to know."

"How does it work?"

"That depends," Babe said. "It depends on visibility—on whether it's night or day; whether or not they're using search-lights; how thick the ack-ack is—a lot of things."

"Can you give me an example?"

"I guess so," Babe said. He stubbed out his cigarette. "The last time we were over Kahili the visibility wasn't very good. We had to come low to see what was in the harbor and then their searchlights went on and the ack-ack started breaking all around us. There were some B-17s at 25,000 feet and they got in the searchlights."

"How do their searchlights work?"

"Sound," Babe said. "The heavier drone of the 17s drew some of the lights away from us. I was at 1,500 feet and I saw a new bunch of lights open up just below me, so I nosed over and dropped my egg."

"How heavy was it?"

"Two thousand pounds," Babe said. "My diving angle was about fifty degrees. I couldn't miss."

"Do you use a bombsight?"

"Not for that. It's just knowing when to let go."

"Practice, then."

"Yes. But the Squadron's flying too much to practice any more," Babe said.

"And Forsyth torpedoed a ship in the harbor?"

"Yes," Babe said. "It was a ship or a big barge. I was getting out too fast to get a good look."

"Is he getting a decoration?" O'Bannon asked, his pencil poised.

"Why?" Babe asked. "He did only what he was supposed to."

O'Bannon looked surprised. "I thought you guys got a medal every time you sank a ship."

"No," Babe said. "That's the Army."

"Don't the Army sink any ships?"

"Not from 25,000 feet at night," Babe said.

"How about daytime?"

Babe shrugged his shoulders. "Their ships are moving during daylight," he said. "Have you ever looked at a ship from 25,000 feet?"

"No," O'Bannon said.

"It looks small," Babe said, "very small. From 5,000 feet they might have a chance of hitting it, but not from five times that height."

"Well," O'Bannon said, "this ain't no time to argue about that. I'd like to know some more about Forsyth. If he ain't getting a medal, it kind of wrecks the story, though."

"He's twenty-five," Babe said, "unmarried, and a hell of a nice guy."

"No wife, huh?" O'Bannon said. "That's too bad. People like to read about fliers doing things for their wives. Maybe he's got a girl."

"If he has," Babe said, "I don't know her name." He reached inside his shirt pocket and brought out his cigarettes. The cellophane wrapping was limp with moisture.

"Got another?"

Babe handed the pack to the correspondent.

"They're hard to get now," O'Bannon said, "and I haven't had a cigar since I left Noumea."

"We're issued a carton a week," Babe said. He waited for the other to find a match and heard Forsyth walking up to the tent.

Forsyth opened the screen door and it banged behind him. "Hello," he said, as he saw the correspondent.

O'Bannon rose and extended his hand. "I'm O'Bannon, of the Washington papers. Your pal's been telling me about you."

Forsyth looked quickly at Babe. "What kind of scuttlebutt have you been passing around?"

"He ain't told me much," O'Bannon said jovially. He sat down again on Forsyth's bunk. "I want to get your story about sinking that ship the other night."

"How'd you hear about it?"

"Your Public Relations Officer told me. That's his job."

"What do you want to know?"

"The whole story. What it felt like. Your reactions—anything you can think of. Are you sure you won't get a medal?"

"Yes," Forsyth said. "I'm sure I won't."

"Maybe the story would help."

"Then I'd rather not tell it," Forsyth said. "You'd better see Phil Jackson. He got a Jap destroyer two weeks ago. He'll have a good story for you."

"The AP guy got that story," he said. "It's old stuff now."

"The Japs are just as dead," Forsyth said. "That's what counts."

"From a news angle, the story's cold," O'Bannon said. "I can't tell the same story every day."

"Then you'd better go back to Honolulu," Forsyth said.

"Why?" O'Bannon looked surprised.

"Because it's the same story here every day. There's nothing different—some planes don't get back, or we sink a ship or Charlie drops some eggs on us. There's no difference between days. They may look different, but they're all the same."

"Are you kiddin'?" O'Bannon asked in amazement.

"No," Forsyth said. "It's the truth. If you want to know what it's like, come up to Kahili with us tonight. There's some more ships off Buin."

"I can't do that," O'Bannon said. "I'm a married man. I got kids."

"A lot of us are married," Forsyth said. "I'm not, but I know guys who are. It doesn't worry them. They never hold back when there's a job to do. They figure they can get back to their wives and their kids that much sooner."

"Don't hold it against me, kid," O'Bannon said, getting up and putting his notebook away. "I just can't afford to take the risks. I spent too long coverin' night courts and doin' rewrite work. This is my chance. It won't do me much good if I get killed."

"That's your problem," Forsyth said. "Figure it out for yourself. The offer still stands. I'll fly you up to Kahili tonight. You might get a whale of a story."

"How far away is it?" he asked, taking off his glasses.

"Three hundred miles," Forsyth said. He sat down and started to take off his forty-five.

"It's too far," O'Bannon said. "I don't swim so good."

"Suit yourself," Forsyth said. "If you'll excuse us now, we have to put on our dinner jackets.'

O'Bannon looked from Forsyth to Babe. He walked over to the door. "Thanks for the cigarette, kid," he said nervously. "I got to be gettin' back to camp."

"Have a good rest," Forsyth said. "Maybe some of the boys will tell you about it in the morning."

The door closed and he was gone. Forsyth put his hands on the cot and looked at Babe. "The bastard," he said. "I used to think those guys were heroes. But he's the kind who always has an excuse for not going on a strike—got a cold or sinus trouble, or his malaria's bad again. How can they write about it if they don't know what it's like?"

"I didn't like him," Babe said.

Forsyth took off his shirt and started out of the door for the wash bench. Babe followed him outside.

"Was there any mail?" he asked.

"I don't know," Eliot said. He poured some water from the can into his helmet. "Ben was going to get it, but he got sidetracked."

Babe found a piece of soap on the bench and poured out some water into the other helmet. He began to wash his hands.

Eliot was sloshing water over his face, trying to rinse off the soap. "Ben's a lucky guy," he said.

"Why?"

"To have that nurse in love with him."

"What nurse?" Babe asked, washing his hands.

"The one who flew in this morning. Evacuating stretcher patients."

"Did he know her a long time?"

"I guess so," Forsyth said. "Wish I could have seen her—or any other woman. I'm getting tired of nothing but baritone voices around me."

"Sometimes when I'm sleeping, it seems like I can hear Marge talking to me," Babe said. "But it makes it worse, when I wake up."

Forsyth dried his face on a dirty turkish towel. "You're lucky," he said. "A guy like you doesn't have to make long-distance calls."

They both laughed and Forsyth went over and hung his towel on the wire. He felt Babe's drying laundry.

"It's coming along," he said. "Should be dry early this afternoon."

"That's good," Babe said, rinsing his face. "I'll need them tomorrow."

When he went into the tent, he thought about the strike.

Afternoon

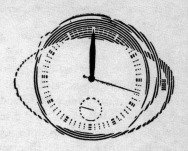

McRae OPENED THE DOOR OF THE MESS HALL AND SAW THAT it was almost filled with officers. He put his gloves into the hip pocket of his shorts and walked to his table at the end of the room. The others at the table were already eating when he got there.

"Commander Knucklehead, I presume," Cordell said.

"Hello, Joe. Anything happen while I was gone?"

"Not a thing. How was the hop?"

"No complaints," McRae said. He swallowed an atabrine pill. "They're certainly a dull bunch at Russell."

"Anybody we know?"

"No," McRae said. "They're having a hell of a time over there. Charlie killed fourteen cattle when he came over two nights ago. One of the men just found the carcasses on a hillside. They're too far gone to eat."

"I'd like to see them first before I turned them down," one of the officers said. "The meat might be a little high, but I bet it'd make good steaks."

"Steaks," Cordell said. "For Christ's sake, don't talk about that." He helped himself from the metal dish of dehydrated potatoes. "Do you remember those breakfasts in Sydney, Larry?"

"I certainly do," McRae said. "Pass the powdered eggs, please."

"Big rump steaks," Cordell said, "smothered with a couple of dozen fresh eggs. Hot cereal and toast. Orange juice and papayas. Toast, coffee, cocoa and milk."

"Milk," McRae said. "I'd give fifty dollars for a glass right now." He smacked his lips suggestively and poured himself another cup of water. "Is there any salt for the eggs?" he asked. He looked at the brown, putty-thick mass on his plate.

"No salt today," one of the officers said, "and no pepper and no bananas."

McRae poured a cup of coffee from the heavy china pitcher. "I'll try to wash them down," he said. "If there was only some way to make them tasteless." He took a forkful of eggs and then a gulp of black coffee. "No," he said, after a moment. "A rotten egg's a rotten egg. I guess there's no way to hide the taste." He pushed aside his plate. "Pass the bread and jam, Joe."

One of the SBD pilots spoke to him from the next table. "How's the strip at Russell, Larry?"

"A little better," McRae said, taking a piece of bread. "It'll improve now that the rains have gone."

"I hope so," the pilot said. "It was lousy before."

"We'll have Charlie's field at Munda after a while," McRae said. "Then Russell won't mean so much."

"Charlie builds nice airfields," the pilot said.

"He did a good job on Henderson." McRae put his knife into the butter bowl and took out a chunk of the hard yellow wax. He began to butter the piece of thick granular bread in his hand. "How was the strike this morning?" he asked.

"Pretty good. There's a recon plane over the strip now. We ought to get the pictures this afternoon."

"Anybody missing?"

"Just one. Ensign Jenkins."

"I didn't know him," McRae said. "What happened?"

"He didn't pull out of his dive soon enough. The flak caught him and his plane blew up at 200 feet."

"New man?"

"Yes," the pilot said. "He'd been with us three weeks."

"That's long enough to learn," McRae said.

"He didn't learn fast enough," the pilot said. "Now he doesn't have to worry about it any more."

"That's right," Cordell said. "At least he's out of the war."

"That's the easy way to stop your troubles," McRae said. He ate the bread and jam. The SBD pilot turned away and talked to the officers at his table.

"Did anybody send Burton's gear home?" McRae asked.

"I think so," Cordell said. "It went to his mother."

"Was there very much?"

"Just his sea chest," Cordell said, "his uniforms and diary and a few souvenirs. He didn't have much."

"Why was he so quiet?" McRae asked. "I never knew him very well."

"He was supporting his mother," one of the officers said. "He was worried about getting knocked off on account of her."

"I wonder what she'll do with his uniforms when she gets them," McRae said. "They won't be much good to anybody."

"She'll probably just look at them," Cordell said, "or hang them in his closet and touch them now and then and pretend he's coming back to wear them again."

"My mother's dead," McRae said. "She's beyond any torture like that."

"Where's your wife, Larry?" Cordell asked.

"She's married again," McRae said. "She's living on a ranch near Los Angeles with her husband."

"You left the Navy because of her, didn't you?"

"Yes," McRae said. "She wanted more than a j.g. could afford."

"You made plenty at Curtiss."

"Enough for a normal woman. But after a while she said she was worried that I'd crack up. What she was really worried about was that she wouldn't be able to spend my money any more. One night when she was drunk she admitted it. I let her divorce me for mental cruelty."

"That was tough," Joe said.

"It wasn't so bad," Larry said. "After a while I didn't think about it any more." He poured himself another cup of coffee.

"This was a lousy meal," Cordell said, wiping his mouth with the back of his hand. "I suppose it's time to start riding the mess treasurer again."

"Take it easy on him, Joe," McRae said. "It's not his fault we aren't getting anything."

"Whose fault is it, Larry?"

"I don't know," McRae said, finishing his coffee. "It's like so many other things. Something's wrong and nobody ever knows why or who's to blame. If there was any food on the island, we'd all get a share of it."

"Yeah," Cordell said, "If we got there first."

"You can always draw a K-Ration from Sick Bay," McRae said.

"They'll be running out some day," Cordell said. "They can't feed the whole squadron."

The flight surgeon came over to McRae's table. "Hello, Larry," he said. "Rotten lunch, wasn't it?"

"Sit down, Doc," McRae said. "What's on your mind?"

"I want Burns grounded for a while," the doctor said. "He's had the shakes ever since that last strike. If I can keep him out of the air for a while, there's a chance he may fly again. Right now he couldn't drive a kiddy-car."

"Whatever you say, Tom," McRae said. "Anything special to blame?"

"I don't think so," the flight surgeon said. "He's just had too much of it for a while."

"What if the shakes don't stop?"

"He'll have to have leave," the doctor said. "Maybe a week in Auckland."

"That would fix up anybody," Cordell said. "Look how my hand trembles. I can hardly light a cigarette."

"Or pull a cork," the doctor said. "You're just hung over."

"How about a hop up the Slot tonight, Doc?" Cordell said. "We'll take a look at *your* hands in the morning."

"No, thanks." The doctor grinned. "I have to be here to take care of whoever gets back."

"If any," Cordell said.

"Yes," the doctor said, "if any."

McRae looked around the mess hall and saw that some of his pilots were starting to leave. He rapped sharply on the coffee pitcher with his spoon and the mess hall became quiet as the men stopped talking. The Squadron Commander stood up.

"I have a brief message for the gentlemen of VTB Eleven," he said. The SBD pilots turned away.

"As you may have heard, there will be a strike at Kahili tonight, weather permitting. Strike briefing will be at four this afternoon. I advise you to get as much sleep as you can before tonight's operation, but don't sleep through the briefing. It's particularly important today. Thank you." He seated himself and felt for a cigarette.

Conversation began in the mess hall again and some of the SBD pilots left.

Babe Lewis came up to McRae. "Sir," he said, "I'd like to go up Kokumbona for some souvenirs this afternoon."

"Go ahead," McRae said. "Be sure you're over at Strike Command by four."

"Thank you, sir. I'll be back by then." He turned and walked quickly down the aisle.

McRae lighted his cigarette and watched his pilots. Some were tracing diagrams on the bare table top with their knife points. Others were sitting, looking out of the side of the mess hall, or smoking or talking across the tables.

Paul Scott walked over to him. "Commander," he said, "it looks like Charlie will be over about three o'clock. Will your planes be dispersed then?"

"Yes," McRae said. "They'll be in their revetments."

"The fighters should be able to intercept over Russell," Scott said. "I thought you'd like to know."

"Thanks," McRae said. "I'm usually the last to hear."

Scott went away and he motioned to Forsyth, who was just leaving the table.

"Any mail come in this morning, Eliot?"

"Don't know yet, sir. A C-47 came in, but I was over at the revetment. Lambert said he'd find out, but the nurse on the plane was an old playmate of his. He never got around to the mail after he saw her."

"That's a funny one," McRae said. "He must have thought it was manna dropping from heaven."

"Or mamma," Forsyth punned. "Anyway, I'll go over to SCAT later and see if there's any mail for us."

"Thanks," McRae said. "I'd even welcome a V-Mail letter now."

"So would I," Forsyth said. "I'm beginning to think they've forgotten we're out here."

"They probably haven't forgotten. They're just getting used to the idea. I guess this place doesn't have the magic name it used to."

"No," Forsyth said. "That's the way it goes. I guess people want to forget about it."

"How do you feel these days?"

"Pretty good," Eliot said. "I'm okay as long as I take my atabrine like a little man."

"Lewis is going up to Kokumbona this afternoon."

"What for?"

"Souvenirs," McRae said. "He probably wants a helmet or a flag to send home."

"I'll tell him where to find them," Forsyth said. "I understand there's a chance we may get Barnes back."

"So I hear. I wonder how he is."

"He should be back tomorrow morning, if they send the Cat out for him."

"Maybe he'll be here for breakfast," McRae said. "I hope they can find him."

"They've a pretty good idea where he is."

"How about his crew?"

Forsyth shook his head. "No word," he said. "He was probably the only one who could get out."

McRae turned a little so that he could look out of the screened windows toward the edge of the clearing. "I wonder sometimes if it isn't better to die quickly than to find yourself on a reef with a couple of holes in you and no food and malaria coming on."

"It's a chance," Forsyth said. "I'd take it."

"I'm older than you," McRae said. "If things looked pretty black, I wonder if I'd think it worth while to try to live."

"I think you would, Larry," Forsyth said. "I don't even know about myself. I don't think anybody can until the time comes. It's soon enough then to find out."

"I think you're right, lad," McRae said. "We never know until it happens. Our responses are so completely conditioned to flying and dropping torpedoes that I wonder if we've got any normal reactions left."

"Probably a few," Forsyth smiled. "I'd like to get down to Sydney or Auckland to find out. I think I'll break out in a sweat at the sight of the first girl."

"Maybe we'll all go together," McRae said. "We rate leave all right, but I hate to say anything about it, just in case it's not on the books for us."

"I know," Forsyth said. "I always kill any scuttlebutt I hear about being relieved."

"It's a pleasant thought, just the same," McRae said. He got up from the table and Eliot followed him down the aisle. Most of the other officers had left. They could hear the noisy clatter of the Filipinos and the colored boys in the galley— fighting over the food, Forsyth thought.

McRae put on his cap and pulled his gloves from his hip pocket. He held them in one hand as though they were a swagger stick while he and Eliot walked between the palms to the path.

They passed the tents of the officers and saw that some of them were asleep already. Others were reading in their cots or writing letters on V-Mail paper. A j.g. was filling his canteen at the Lister bag that swung from an iron tripod. In the distance they could hear a young tenor voice singing a song, the tune of which corresponded roughly to "I Want a Girl."

As they walked nearer, other voices joined in and they heard the men singing:

"I wanted wings, and I got the god-damned things.
Now I don't want them any more.
They taught me how to fly and they sent me here to die;
I've had a bellyful of war."

Forsyth looked at McRae. "They're singing that again," he said.

"Yeah," McRae said. "The Song of the Solomons."

They passed the tent where the men were singing and as they walked farther the mocking words came after them:

"You can leave the Zeros to the god-damned heroes;
Distinguished Fly-ing Crosses—
Do not compensate for losses. . ."

"Yes," Forsyth said, as they stopped in front of McRae's tent. "The Song of the Solomons."

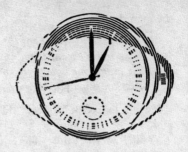

*W*HEN FORSYTH CAME TO HIS TENT HE SAW THAT BABE WAS sitting on the steps, cleaning his carbine.

"You're off to the hills, I hear," Eliot said.

"Yes," Babe said. "I want some souvenirs to send home."

"There's plenty around. Why don't you trade for them?"

"It wouldn't be the same. Besides, I haven't anything to trade."

"That's true," Forsyth said. "But, with a quart of liquor, you could get anything."

"How about a *hara-kiri* knife?"

"For a quart," Eliot said, "you could get a dozen." He edged past Babe and went into the tent.

Babe rubbed the excess oil from the barrel with a piece of an old skivvy shirt. "Why don't you come along, Eliot?"

"No, thanks," Forsyth said from inside the tent. "I've done it before. You can bring me back a thigh bone, if you feel like it. My knife needs a new handle."

"Glad to," Babe said. He finished rubbing the carbine and laid it across his knee. He wondered how he would be able to tell a thigh bone from any other bone—probably be a big one.

"Who're you going with?"

"Some Marines," Babe said. "Fellow I knew in Indiana."

"Are they going out for snipers?"

"I think he did say something about that," Babe said. "Are there many?"

"A few," Forsyth said. "They're back in the hills, starving to death, and every now and then we kill a few more. I'd like to see you get those bastards up there with the searchlight."

"Where is it?" Babe asked.

"Christ," Forsyth said, "if we knew, we could strafe them or dive-bomb the light. Whenever they send over a lot of planes at night, it comes on. Shows Charlie the way to Henderson."

"I didn't know that."

"There are a hell of a lot of odd things here," Forsyth said. "Better stick close to the Gyrenes when you get in the jungle. It'll be safer."

"What're you going to do?"

"Sleep," Forsyth said. "We'll probably have Condition Red this afternoon. I'm going to try to sleep through it. We've got a big night ahead of us."

"I'm still hungry," Babe said. "I didn't get hardly anything to eat."

"We all feel the same," Forsyth said. "Better draw a K-Ration to take with you. You'll get hungry as hell after you've walked a while."

"How about water?"

"Two canteens," Forsyth said. "You'll want one each way. Have you had malaria yet?"

"I don't know," Babe said. "I'm taking atabrine."

"You've got it all right. Don't bother about helmet netting. You'd better wear a flight suit. The vines would tear your bare legs to shreds."

"I've got an old one I can wear," Babe said.

"You're not in condition for a pull up Kokumbona," Forsyth said. "Take it easy. Don't forget to be over at Strike Command by four."

"I'll be back in time," Babe said. He got up and opened the door of the tent. He went inside and laid the gun on his unmade bunk.

"That's a nice gun," Forsyth said. "I wish I could get one like it."

"I got it at Pearl," Babe said. He took off his shorts and shirt and reached for the greasy brown flight suit that hung from a nail in back of his cot.

"That's the way it always is," Forsyth said, lying down on his bunk. "The jokers back home always get the best equipment. We never see it out here."

"We all had them at Ford Island," Babe said, closing the leg zippers on his suit. It was a light material, resembling gabardine—the first one that had been issued him. He took his knife sheath from the bed and put it on the webbed weapons belt.

"Here's my canteen," Forsyth said. "I just filled it. The chlorine hasn't even had a chance to settle yet."

"Thanks," Babe said. He sat down on his bunk and put the other canteen on the belt. Then he took off the .45 holster and put it under his pillow. A jeep horn honked harshly outside the tent and he stood up and looked out.

"Here they are," he said. He fastened the belt around his waist and took the carbine from the bed. The liner of his helmet was on the table and he put it on his head. "See you later," he said.

"So long, Stanley," Forsyth said. "Don't forget the femur for me—without ants."

"I'll bring one back," Babe said. The horn brayed again

and he went out of the tent. A lieutenant was driving and there were two enlisted men in the rear seat.

"Wait a second," Babe called. He went to the wash bench and got his helmet. He crammed it over the pressed plastic liner and walked over to the jeep. "Hello, Bud," he said. "I'm all set now."

"Get in," the Marine lieutenant said. "This is Evans and Meiklejohn—Ensign Lewis."

"Afternoon, sir," the Marines said.

"Hello," Babe said. "Are we all set?"

"All set," the lieutenant said. "Let's go." He put the jeep into low and, as it moved ahead, he turned and drove it over to the road.

They had been walking along the trail for ten minutes before it turned up the side of the mountain. The lieutenant went first, followed by Corporal Evans and then Babe and, after him, Meiklejohn. The trail was about six inches wide and at hip height it was arched with long saw-grasses. Above them, thin wiry vines trailed down from branches of the jungle trees. As they went deeper into the jungle, the atmosphere changed. There was no breeze and the air was still and fetid. Babe could feel the sweat rolling down his chest. He pushed his helmet back and wiped his forehead. The jungle was very quiet and Babe found that he had a tendency to try to walk without noise. The trunk of a tree blocked the trail and they climbed over it. Babe's carbine caught in a vine and nearly slipped from his shoulder. The webbed belt wore into his hips and the two canteens slapped his buttocks like saddlebags. He felt for his knife and found that it was still in its sheath. He began to want a cigarette and then he realized that the sweat from his lips would drown it before he had taken four drags.

He wiped his face with the back of his hand. Mosquitoes buzzed near by.

"How you doin', Babe?" the lieutenant called back.

"Pretty good, Bud. I haven't walked for a long time." He could feel the muscles in his calf begin to tighten. His feet felt hot and he knew that they were beginning to swell.

A moment later Corporal Evans pointed to the side of the trail. "We're getting there," he said. "There's one of their gas masks."

Babe peered under the foliage as he passed and saw a yellow-brown face mask on the ground. The rubber was rotten and the metal cannister was speckled with rust.

"They brought gas," Evans said. "I wonder why they never used it."

"I guess they were afraid to," Meiklejohn said.

"Babe," the lieutenant called back, "take a look around. . . . No cocoanut trees."

"Where are they?" Babe asked. He had not noticed the absence of palms.

"Down below us. They don't grow up this high." His voice echoed dully in the hot air.

Babe could feel his heart begin to pound. His head was wet with sweat and the back of his flight suit slapped wetly against him as he walked. He unscrewed the cap of his canteen.

"Have you got salt pills, sir?" Meiklejohn asked.

"No," Babe said, "I forgot them."

Meiklejohn slung his rifle over his shoulder and reached inside his trousers pocket. He handed two pills to Babe.

Babe swallowed them and screwed on the canteen top. He put it away in its case on his hip, and bent low to get under some branches that crossed the trail. He kept the muzzle of his carbine pointing upward so that no dirt would get in the barrel. He could hear Bud climbing through the bush away from the trail and he looked up but could not see him. Ahead of him, Evans turned off the trail and slung his rifle over his shoulder, then pushed the vines apart and dug his feet into the steep bank. Babe followed him and put his feet in the holes in the soft humus that the others' feet had made. He had to grab some roots to pull himself up, and work along on his knees and toes, and, finally, when he had climbed the dozen feet under the thick vines, he looked around and saw Bud bending over, looking into a big hole that had been dug into the side of the hill. Some poles had been stuck into the ground outside and another one joined them five feet from the ground. It looked like the kind of lean-to shelter he had learned to build at camp. Vines had been twisted around the joints and branches had formed a little roof, but now that had fallen through and trash littered the level place in front of the cave.

"Here it is," Bud said. "Six of them lived here until we killed them."

Babe rested on his carbine and looked around. There was a cooking pit just under the edge of the lean-to and the damp rocks that lined it were blackened with smoke. To the right of the shelter some lengths of wood had been cut and stacked. Shoes, cocoanut husks, pieces of netting, kidney-shaped aluminum mess kits, leather harness, wads of paper and a few bones were scattered in front of the hole. He bent over the cooking pit and saw that scraps of cocoanut shell were lying near it. There was no meat on any of the pieces and he could see that they had been scraped clean.

"Did they bring the cocoanuts with them?" he asked.

"Yes," Bud said. "When they knew they were going to hide in the jungle they got cocoanuts and dragged them up here with netting. Then they ate them. They cut open the cocoanuts and ate the meat and gnawed the shells like rats. They boiled drinking water in their canteens."

"Was that all they had?"

"Just about. Some of them had canned rations, but not very many. See," he said, pointing with his foot, "there's a bird's skull. Something they shot and cooked and picked clean."

Babe saw a canteen half covered with dead leaves. He leaned over and picked up its leather strap. The slimy leather came apart in his hand. He drew back and turned the canteen over with the butt of his carbine and the leather case fell off. Some red ants ran across the side of the smoke-darkened water bottle. He wondered what was inside the cave, and started to walk toward the opening.

"Don't go in there," Bud said. "There's just a few moldy blankets and some rotten clothing. You'll get yourself filthy."

Babe picked his way through the things on the ground.

"Look there," Evans said.

Babe saw that he was pointing at something near the wood-pile. He went over to it and saw the rusty hobnails of the sole of a shoe and something attached to it that looked like a wet log. He touched it with his toe and a piece of legging fell off. Ants poured out of the inside of the leg, swarming crazily over the rotten cloth, and then went back through the place where he had bared the tibia. Babe drew away a little and looked at Evans.

"They'll have that leg finished off in another week," he said. "I bet there's nothin' inside the shoe right now." He poked it with his rifle butt and it collapsed hollowly. The decayed leather tore a little where the butt had pressed on it.

"Here's a helmet," Bud said. He kicked the rusty bowl of metal toward Babe. It rang tinnily and stopped near his feet.

Babe picked it up and looked at it. The leather inside was rotten and falling out. Some netting still clung to the outside. A tin star was centered on the thin helmet.

"What's the star for?" he asked.

"I'm not sure," Bud said. "They all had them. I never saw a Jap helmet that didn't have one."

"I guess it means private," Private Meiklejohn said. He picked up a canteen and pulled out the cork. Dirty water trickled out and splattered on the wet leaves.

"Anything you want here?" Bud asked. "There's some better stuff ahead."

"What kind of stuff?" Babe asked.

"Oh, grenades and machine-gun ammo; rifles and Lugers, map cases—flags. We'll do better up at the next place."

"How about bones?" Babe asked.

"That's what we got the most of," the lieutenant said. "What do you want—skulls?"

"No," Babe said, "just a thigh bone."

"Plenty of them." the lieutenant said.

"The guy I'm living with wants one for a knife handle."

Evans spoke up. "Tell him to split it and dry it in the sun good," he said. "Then he can scrape it and get it down to size and when he puts it on the knife it won't warp."

Babe looked at the helmet again and decided to leave it there. If he couldn't find a better one at the next place he could pick up this one on the way back. He dropped it on the soft earth and it rolled in a semi-circle and stopped a few feet away.

"Let's go back to the trail," the lieutenant said. He turned and went slowly down the side of the hill, holding on to creepers and roots and then Evans went down and Babe shifted his carbine to his other shoulder and climbed after them, digging his heels into the wet earth and leaning backward so that he would not fall.

Then they were on the path again and he could hear Private Meiklejohn behind him, pushing aside branches as they went along the trail.

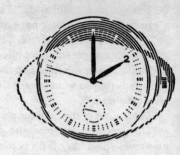

*C*ORDELL SAT ON HIS COT, CHECKING HIS FLIGHT LOG, WHEN there was a knock on his door.

"Come in," he said, turning around. A young pilot came into the tent.

"I'm Griffin, sir," the pilot said. "Reporting for duty with the Squadron."

"Glad to have you with us," Cordell said. He got up and they shook hands. "When'd you get in?"

"Just flew in on SCAT."

"Where've you been?"

"New Cal," Griffin said. He sat down on the chair.

"Got all your gear?"

"Yes," Griffin said. "I brought it all with me."

"There's not enough planes for all of us," Cordell said. "We take turns."

"How often do you fly?"

"Pretty regularly," Cordell said. "It keeps us busy."

"I left my gear up at Hotel de Gink," Griffin said. "Will I get quarters down here later?"

"Yes. Maybe there'll be something for you tomorrow."

86

"Why tomorrow?"

"We're flying tonight," Cordell said. "There's a strike at Kahili."

"Is that far?"

"Three hundred miles up the Slot," Cordell said. "Course: Two Nine Three."

"Will I be going?"

"Not tonight," Cordell said. "Not for a few nights. Don't worry about it. You'll have all the flying you can handle after a while."

"I hope so," Griffin said. "I've been waiting for it a long time."

"When did you leave Pearl?"

"A month ago," the new pilot said. "I've been on every island between there and here. It got damned tiresome."

"It's the same here," Cordell said. "It doesn't take long to get tired of it."

"Do you want my orders?"

"Yes. I'm the exec, for the time being anyway. I'll get them endorsed for you. Why don't you go back to de Gink and take it easy? You'll meet the rest of the boys at dinner."

"Thanks," Griffin said. He got up from the table and gave Cordell an envelope full of papers. "Whose place am I taking?" he asked.

"That's a funny question," he said. "The kid's name was Burton."

"I just wondered," Griffin said.

Cordell smoothed the envelope and put it on the top of the table. "We're being briefed for tonight's strike at sixteen hundred," he said. "You might like to sit in."

"I would," Griffin said.

"It'll be at Strike Command. Anybody can point it out to you."

"I'll be there," Griffin said. "Will the skipper be around?"

"Yes," Cordell said. "You'll meet him then."

"Can I get a cup of coffee anywhere?"

"Yes," Cordell said. "Over at the mess hall. It's the big Quonset hut in the clearing."

"Right," Griffin said. "See you at Strike Command." He went out of the tent and Cordell opened up his flight log again. He added a column of figures on a piece of scrap paper and held it up and looked at it. So far this month he had flown more than one hundred hours.

Lambert felt somebody pushing his shoulder and he opened his eyes. It was Scott standing beside his cot.

"Wake up, Ben," he said. "This is a big afternoon."

Lambert sat up. "What's happening?"

"Charlie's coming down the Slot," Paul said.

"What of it? I want to sleep."

"You're out of luck. They'll be sounding Condition Red. The fighters are gassing up now."

"Where're you going?"

"Over to Strike," Paul said. "You better come, too. Enjoy life at its best. You can sleep in the corner if you want. I've got Fighter Director duty."

"Sure," Lambert said. "I'll come over." He sat on the edge of his cot and felt for his shoes.

"I understand a friend of yours flew in this morning," Scott said. "What luck!"

"Looking permitted, but do not handle," Lambert said. "It's a hell of a place to run into a girl you know."

"I wouldn't mind," Scott said, "except that my wife might care." He picked up Ben's weapons belt and gave it to him.

"Hear from her often?"

"She writes every day."

88

"What does she say?"

"The same things."

"Like what?"

Scott grinned. "None of your business. Get married yourself and find out."

"Nope," Lambert said. "I can't spare the time."

"Is that all?"

"Theres more than just that," he said. "When you're flying it makes a difference."

"I know how you feel," Scott said. He picked up the empty Burgundy bottle that held the candle. "Penfold's Wines," he said. "From Australia?"

"Yes," Lambert said. "Sydney. That was the last time I saw her."

"Who?"

"The nurse," Lambert said. "You know damn well who I mean." He picked up his cap and sun glasses from the table.

"Got everything?"

"Yeah. C'mon."

They went out of the tent and Lambert pulled the screen door shut, so that the flies would not get inside. Scott drove the jeep over to Henderson and parked it a hundred yards from Strike Command in the dispersal area. The B-17s and B-24s were being pulled over to the edge of the jungle into camouflaged revetments. Men were walking across the runway, dispersing the dive bombers and the Hudsons. Soon, only the fighters would be left. Lambert saw a gas truck drive across the taxi mat and turn up a path that led into the jungle. "They're really getting set," he said.

"They've learned," Scott said. "Everything stops for Charlie."

Inside Strike Command there were about a dozen officers and twice that number of enlisted men. Some of them were seated at drawing boards. Others wore headphones and were testing the Fighter Director liaison. Lambert went to the thermos jug and drank a cup of water.

Scott spoke to the officer in charge. "What's the situation, sir?" he asked.

"The cruisers are between Savo and Florida," he said. "The Bogies have left Vila, heading for Russell."

"How many?"

"Around ninety," the officer said. "Reconnaissance says about half of them are torpedo planes, a quarter medium bombers and the rest fighters."

"Can we break them up?"

"I think so."

"Any planes in the air?"

"Yes. The P-38s are orbiting at 20,000 between Russell and Esperance. The Corsairs are 5,000 feet lower at fifteen. The Wildcats are at 10,000 and the P-40s cover from there to the ground."

"What's the plan?"

"Their medium bombers will probably come in over Henderson to knock out the runway and try to suck our fighters away from Esperance. If they do, the torpedo planes can go in after our cruisers. Don't let your group leave Esperance. We can always patch up Henderson; cruisers are a little harder."

"How about dogfights?"

"For God's sake, don't let any of them get sucked into single combat. The Zeros may look easy to the kids, but if they go after one they're out of the play. Charlie may get a touchdown."

"Right," Scott said. He turned away and saw that Lambert was sitting on a stool in the corner, reading a magazine.

"What've you got, Ben?"

"*Superman*," Lambert said. He held up the colored comic magazine. "I love him."

"This may be a long afternoon."

"I'm ready for it," Lambert said. "I've got *Dick Tracy* too." He pulled another magazine from under his rump. "Let it rain, let it pour. This steel-fish jockey ain' gwine worry no more."

Scott laughed. "The hell with you," he said. "I'm not gonna worry about you either. Stand clear, man. I've got work to do."

"There's no hurry," Lambert said. "Take it easy while you can. Why don't you establish your liaison channel and then wait for them? The fighter boys will see Charlie before you do. The warning system will give you plenty of time."

"I wish I could be as unconcerned as that," Scott said. "You're used to it. Besides, it doesn't make much difference to you."

"That's right," Lambert said. "If we shot them all down or didn't get any, it wouldn't make much difference to me. I wouldn't like to have them get the cruisers, but, even if they did, it wouldn't change my life much."

"What about the men who'd be killed?" Scott said.

"We couldn't hear them scream from here," Ben said. "You and I couldn't see the flames and the smoke and the ships going down and the oil on the water. It's easy to write them off from here. If I were flying this afternoon, it would be different, but my job's tonight. Right now it's up to the boys in the Pea-shooters. Tonight it's my turn."

"Don't you have any feeling for them?"

"I suppose so," Ben said. "But I've seen a lot of it, Paul. It doesn't change very much. You sink a ship or you shoot a plane down and the war still goes on. Charlie still has a navy and a lot of planes to throw at us whenever he gets mad. I can't get hysterical each time we lose a cruiser or a sub or a fighter. It happens all the time, but it's not my business because I take my orders from Larry McRae and we fly up the Slot to kill or sink or disable whatever we can." He tilted back his baseball cap.

"Did you always feel that way?"

"No," Ben said, "not until I was at Pearl Harbor and Midway and the Coral Sea and North Africa."

"What happened over there?"

"Our ships began the bombardment at daybreak. We had all their shore batteries located and we pounded hell out of them. One of our old four-stackers slipped into the harbor to beach the assault troops and was blown up by a mine. I saw it turn over on the men who were struggling in the water with heavy packs and I guess most of them drowned.

"Early in the afternoon we saw white flags over the town and then some French officers came down to the beach and surrendered. After that we went ashore on liberty and drank at the bars and bought souvenirs from the natives, and the French officers at the bar said of course it was just a question of honor and they were really very glad to have us come, but I couldn't forget the little four-stacker that broke in half and the men in the water trying not to die."

"I'd never forget it either," Scott said. A sergeant came over to him and said something.

"Just a minute, Ben. The group leader wants to talk to me." Scott went over to the other side of the room, finding his way between moving men.

Lambert saw him sit at his drawing board and adjust his headphones. He spoke for a moment through the mike and then crossed the room again.

"Contact report," he said. "They're over Russell."

"Good," Lambert said. "The fun ought to start in about ten minutes."

"Are you staying in here?"

"Not if there's anything to see," Ben said. "If any Bogies get through and make a run at the field, I want to step out for a look. I'm getting sick of ducking my head every time Charlie comes over with a few eggs. He's a rotten shot."

"I've seen nights when he wasn't," Scott said. "I'll stay here, if you don't mind."

"It's a good idea for the guys who bomb to be bombed now and then," Ben said. "It makes us appreciate our jobs."

"There's something in that," Scott said. "Maybe I'll work up courage enough to go on a strike with you some time."

"No," Ben said. "It's not a question of courage; it's a question of not caring. You remember the story about the blind mule?"

"Never heard of it."

"Well, one farmer tried to sell another farmer this blind mule. The second farmer was suspicious and demanded that the mule be turned loose. The owner reluctantly complied and the mule tore away and ran into a barn wall. The second farmer said, 'See! I knew your mule was blind.' 'Blind, hell!' the first farmer said. 'That mule just don't give a damn.' "

"And you're like the blind mule," Scott said.

"Most of us are. We don't give a damn."

"Just the same," Scott said, "it's lucky for guys like me that there are guys like you."

"Maybe it is. I never gave it much thought."

"I have," Paul said. "And they need you a hell of a lot more than they need me."

"Don't be too sure of that," Lambert said. "We can all be replaced."

"Your squadron couldn't," Scott said. "Look at the guys in it."

"Yeah," Lambert said. "Men from the *Yorktown*, the *Lex-*

ington, the *Wasp* and the *Hornet*. Almost all of us have had a carrier shot out from under us; some have had two. They didn't have any other place to put us, so they sent us here."

"That wasn't it," Scott said. "They need you here."

"Maybe they do, at that," Ben said. "I guess we're good guys to have around."

Scott went over to the thermos and filled a cup with the cool water. He took a couple of salt pills from the big jar and refilled the cup and brought it back to Lambert.

"This gets more like the USO every day," Ben said. "You guys'll have a floor show up here next, with cigars and drinks."

"This is the place, all right," Scott said. He waited until Ben had drunk the water and returned the cup. The room was becoming quieter and he saw the other officers sitting at their tables, talking with the planes through the mikes, and the men carrying messages and charts from table to table.

He touched Lambert's shoulder and Ben looked up from the comic book. "The spare helmets are hanging up there," he said. "Help yourself if you want one."

"Thanks," Ben said. "I always forget mine." He could see battered, dusty helmets hanging from a board near the overhead. Nails had been driven into it and the helmets were hanging from their straps. There was a light haze of cigarette smoke hovering near the ceiling and he knew that it would become thicker as the afternoon went by and the men smoked more and threw away the butts nervously.

Now is the time, he thought. Now is the time for all good men to settle down and concentrate on keeping Charlie away from Henderson and the cruisers. He felt a little sorry for the long gray ships that were plowing through Sleepless Lagoon. He hoped they would not be sunk.

Then the loudspeaker crackled into life and they could hear the Army group commander speaking from 20,000 feet above

Cape Esperance. *"Santa Claus to Maryland. Santa Claus to Maryland; Bogies at eighteen thousand. Bearing Two Eight. Bogies at eighteen thousand. Bearing Two Eight. Acknowledge."*

And the senior officer spoke over the mike: *"Maryland to Santa Claus. Maryland to Santa Claus. Roger . . . Roger."*

The officer at the large drafting table drew a long arrow on the chart beginning at the center of Henderson and pointing toward the position of the Jap planes. He took the relative bearing with parallel rules and wrote it quickly on a paper form. A messenger took it to the senior officer.

"All planes," the senior officer said. *"Bogies at eighteen thousand. Bearing Two Eight. Bogies at eighteen thousand. Bearing Two Eight."*

Lambert saw that Scott was talking over the mike. He was watching the chart in front of him and drawing lines of bearing and relative distance.

Lambert picked up the comic magazine from the cement floor where he had dropped it and began looking at the pictures again.

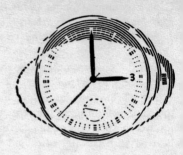

*H*ENDERSON LOOKED DESERTED. LAMBERT SAT ON THE HILL by a row of sandbags outside Strike Command, watching the big white clouds that formed a background for the jungle. Five Corsairs orbited lazily overhead and, as he looked up at them, the chin straps of his helmet grazed against his face. The loud-speaker buzzed harshly inside the operations room, its sounds carrying out to where he sat.

Some P-40s flew low over the palms toward Lunga Point and he knew that they were waiting for the torpedo planes to come into the channel. He wished that he were flying a Corsair or even a Wildcat today. He had finished looking at the comic magazines and now there was nothing to do but wait for the thing to happen. A fighter squadron taxied out to the end of Henderson, ready to take off and meet the one it was relieving. Then the first one would gas up again and stand by to go upstairs. It was tough luck if you were strafed on the ground or the runway was bombed while you were taking off.

Lambert figured the task force must be in the narrowest part of the channel. He looked at his wrist watch and knew that it would be fifteen minutes before they would have enough seaway to maneuver against the Jap planes. Then, far away, over the tip of Cape Esperance, he could see the P-38s streaking to the west and he heard the loudspeaker inside:

"Intercepting Bogies at eighteen thousand. Intercepting Bogies at eighteen thousand. Coming yourwards. Coming yourwards. About twenty-five of them." It went dead again and Ben strained his eyes toward the pencil-thin 38s that were dropping from above. He hoped that some Corsairs would take the Zeros out of the play so that the Lightnings could get to the Mitsubishis without interference. The first flight of Bogies looked like little white pin points against the blue sky as they flew toward Henderson. The first Lightning made a pass at the formation and pulled away. The others followed in turn and then he saw a little puff of smoke, like flak, dropping from the group of bombers. It fell away and streamed down toward the sea. The bombers came on and the Lightnings climbed above them for another pass.

The loudspeaker spoke: *"Scratch one Bogie,"* it said.

He knew that if they got much closer, the fighters would have to break away and let the ack-ack try to stop them. The 38s circled over their target and then winged over, one by one. This time he saw three puffs of smoke drop out of the formation, and one exploded into a blob of orange flame. One Lightning fell slowly, like a brown autumn leaf, toward the channel. Lambert watched to see a parachute blossom out behind it, but there was none and the plane fell crazily until it was out of sight behind the trees. He saw a group of bombers break away from the formation and fly toward some thick clouds. The Lightnings ignored them and climbed again for a third pass at the Mitsubishis.

"Three Bogies minus," the loudspeaker said. *"Lieutenant Weber just crashed into the sea."*

The Lightnings were jockeying for position, flying in an

open echelon of Vees as they overtook the bombers. There were eight Mitsubishis left in the flight, and the Lightnings were above them now, readying for their last pass before the planes reached Henderson.

"*Graveyard to Maryland. Graveyard to Maryland,*" the loudspeaker rasped. "*Twenty Bogies going downstairs for run at cruisers. Bogies . . . run at cruisers. We are intercepting. We are intercepting.*"

Lambert could not see the P-40s, but he knew that the old Kites would be going down to break up the torpedo-plane formation. He could picture what was happening on the cruisers and cans: men standing by the forty- and twenty-millimeter guns, training and depressing until the torpedo planes got within range—the five-inch mounts ready to set up a fixed barrage at 5,000 yards or firing into the water to kick up eighty-foot waterspouts that could smash a plane as though it were made of paper and balsa.

The Lightnings began their last pass at the bombers. They had split into two groups and were dropping alternately on the Mitsubishis from the right and from the left. That way they could make a longer run at a given bomber, confusing the gunners by their constantly changing angle of approach. The flight of bombers that had broken away came out of the clouds again, and Lambert could see that it was heading straight for Henderson. The fighter squadron at the end of the field roared into life, throwing up whirls of dust as the planes followed each other down the runway and into the air. They zoomed past Lambert and headed out toward Sealark Channel. He could hear the whine of the interceptors as they dove on the oncoming bombers and this time he saw one Mitsubishi explode in a blast of debris and two more start to spin down toward the jungle. As the last Lightning finished its run, a fourth bomber caught fire and flew along still in formation, its flames trickling out behind it, until the tail had burned away and it began a slow spin toward the earth.

The remaining four dove steeply and the Lightnings formed up again below them and started to climb. But the bombers were in line with Henderson now and Lambert knew that they would loose their eggs in a moment.

He leaned back against the side of the hill as the four white planes came on and then he heard the eerie whistle of the first bombs as they dropped from the open bays. It always reminded him of the rustle of heavy silk and the pitch rose as they fell closer and he turned over on his stomach and put his hands over the back of his neck and buried his face in the grass. The explosions came far away as the first string hit near the edge of the jungle, and the others came nearer until it sounded as though somebody were pounding irregularly on a tremendous metal drum. He waited for a moment until the rocks had stopped falling. Then he rolled over, shielding his eyes with one hand, and looked up at the sky. The bombers were going away, climbing as they turned. The Lightnings followed them out to sea and he saw that the Corsairs had caught the second flight of bombers over Cape Esperance. A furious dogfight was in progress. Two planes broke away from the milling group and climbed into the sky—a Corsair chasing a Zero. The Corsair gained on the other plane and suddenly the Zero went into a tight skidding turn and the Corsair followed.

Lambert felt his breath quicken. Don't follow him, you damn fool, he thought, but the Corsair finished its wider turn and followed the Zero into the second turn. Both planes had their wings vertical and he could see that the Zero was gaining on the Corsair. Then suddenly the Corsair straightened out and tried to break away, but the Zero followed and Ben could see the white-hot sparks of tracers spanning the little gap of sky between the Zero's nose and the Corsair's tail. The Zero pulled away and spiraled down. A thin streak of blue-gray smoke came from the tail of the Corsair, still flying level. He watched it for a minute and saw that the pilot was climbing out of the cockpit. The Corsair banked gently and the pilot fell away. Lambert saw the little pilot-chute whip out behind him, dragging the silk from the pack, and then the pilot's body jerked as the main umbrella opened.

The chute was drifting down toward Lunga Point, away from the battle, and the Zero followed it down. He saw the Zero level off, a half mile away from the white parasol that swayed like a pendulum over its dark burden below. The Zero flew on toward the drifting chute and, when it was a hundred yards away, the tracer sparks licked out, spraying the chute, and then he could see the pilot's body kick convulsively as the bullets tore through him. The Zero banked away and headed back for Esperance. As it went, little black wool puffs broke beside and above and below it. The plane rolled and climbed and banked as it changed course, trying to escape the tightening claws of the ack-ack. Then the sky was pinpointed with black-and-white dots around the plane and it burst into flame and its nose dropped into a long screaming glide as it turned over on its back and fell toward the jungle.

The torn chute was being carried out over the channel. As he watched it sink lower he heard the sharp bark of the five-inch guns from the cruisers and he knew that the torpedo planes were making a run on the task force. He looked at his watch again and guessed that the ships were through the narrow neck between Florida and Savo and in the wider part of Sealark off Malaita. They would have a better chance now.

Most of the planes had gone from Esperance and he saw that a flight of Wildcats was approaching Henderson for refueling.

There were a few holes on the runway and a big one on the

taxi mat at the far side. At the edge of the jungle a B-17 burned briskly. He could hear the crackling roar as the flames shot up toward the palms and he saw men running away from it and a big gas truck bumping over the narrow path that led to another camouflaged revetment.

"Bogies dispersed," the loudspeaker crackled. The cruisers had stopped firing.

Lambert saw the top of the parachute disappearing below the tops of the palms past Lunga Beach. The first Wildcat had landed and was skidding down the runway, avoiding the bomb craters. The second followed and then the rest in order. One of them caught a wheel in a crater edge and ground looped, smashing the vertical stabilizer. The fighters collected at the end of the field and, looking up again, he could see the Corsairs coming back from Esperance. The P-38s turned in formation and crossed Henderson as they approached Fighter Two. The New Zealand Kites with their white fuselage stripe were circling over Fighter One. The leader dipped down and the others held back for a moment before they leveled off for their approach.

Ben took off his helmet and laid it on the sandbags beside him. The sun felt good on his damp hair. His shirt was wet through and he pulled the tails out so that the air could get to his back. He took off his .45 and lay back on the hill watching the clear blue sky above. The men were talking excitedly inside Strike Command. He tried to listen to them, but the sounds were garbled by the thick walls. He watched the Fortress still burning and saw the rest of the fighters land, and after a while he saw Scott walk out of the sandbagged doorway and stand smoking a cigarette while he looked out over Henderson.

"What's the story?" Ben asked.

"They've gone," Scott said. He came over and sat down beside Lambert. He was shaking a little.

"How many'd we get?"

"About thirty," Scott said. "We won't know until all the fighter pilots have been questioned. They didn't do much damage to the runway, did they?"

"No," Lambert said. "They kicked a few rocks loose and that's about all."

"Where were you?"

"Right here," Ben said. "Thanks for the helmet. I'll bring mine next time."

"Could you see much?"

"I think so. Everything but the cruisers. How'd they make out?"

"Don't know. The Kites broke up the torpedo attack pretty well."

"The New Zealanders are good flyers," Lambert said. "I wish they had some real planes."

"They knocked down half a dozen planes," Scott said. "The other torpedo planes saw what happened and stayed away. Evidently they flew low over Florida, hoping nobody'd see them."

"Did you hear about the parachute?"

"Yes," Scott said thickly, "I did."

"He tried to dogfight," Lambert said. "He thought he could get away with it."

"What a horrible way to be killed!" Scott said. "God!"

"He might have been killed in his plane, too," Lambert said. "He certainly laid himself open for it."

"But he almost lived through it," Scott said. "Christ! To be machine-gunned in your parachute! If the bastard hadn't killed him in cold blood, he might be walking back from it now."

"All killing's in cold blood," Lambert said. "There's no difference."

"I thought it was harder to kill a man if you could see him."

"After a while," Lambert said, "those fine distinctions fade."

Some officers came out of the doorway and walked down the steps. One of them lighted a pipe.

"What's the trouble?" Ben asked. "Why are you so nervous?"

"Just thinking about what happened," Scott said. He pulled some cigarettes from his pocket and threw away the one he had been smoking.

"Sounds like a good afternoon's work," Lambert said. "I don't think we've got any complaints. How many planes did we lose?"

"Seven, I think," Scott said. "Four of ours, two Army and one New Zealand."

"This is a bad day for Charlie." Lambert lighted a cigarette.

"He might have knocked off our cruisers."

"He didn't, though. After a while he'll learn that we're boss around here. From now on the fleet can do pretty much what it wants." He looked down and saw that some dump trucks and scrapers were working on the runway.

"System," he said. "The Nips can't beat system, plus brains."

"No," Paul said, "I know that."

"Now the fleet can work beyond the limit of darkness," Ben said.

"What's that?" Scott asked.

"It's an old fleet doctrine that the striking radius of a task force is limited by the hours of darkness," Ben said.

"I see," Scott said. "Get out of Charlie's range by daylight."

"That's it. Before air power counted for much, they used to figure that in eight hours of darkness a task force could head toward the enemy for four hours before having to turn around and steam back."

"And it's different now."

"Yes," Lambert said. "Now that the cruisers can have air

cover from Henderson, they can go a lot farther. The fighters give them protection the way they did this afternoon. You saw how it worked out."

"What it amounts to, then, is that the limit of darkness is pushed back to the limit of our own air cover."

"Right," Ben said. "That's why we're here—to keep pushing it back."

"I never thought of it that way," Scott said. "Probably because I was never with the fleet."

"The Navy changes," Ben said. "Hell, we all change. Don't worry about not being a salty old Pelican. You're doing a damn good job where you are."

The enlisted men who were coming off watch crowded out of the doorway. Some of them were eating bars of chocolate D-Ration. They went down the hill and stood by the side of the road, thumbing rides back to camp on the trucks that drove past.

"They're a smart bunch of boys," Scott said. "They know what's going on."

"It's their job," Lambert said. "Out here a man is likely to take his job pretty seriously."

"It's damn good to have boys like that to work with," Scott said. "They're all swell."

"The mechs are a good bunch, too," Lambert said. "My plane captain knows more about planes than I'll ever know."

"Does he ever fly with you?"

"Not if the strike's dangerous," Lambert said. "It takes a hell of a lot longer to make a Chief Aviation Machinist's Mate than it does to make a j.g. pilot. He's worth five like me. He never turns in until the plane's ready to go again. I'm whipped after a few hours of flying."

"To Kahili and back," Scott said. He flicked his cigarette down the side of the hill.

"Maybe," Lambert said. He looked over toward the palms at the edge of the clearing and saw that the B-17 was still burning. Little flames licked up around the engines, and where the skin had been burned from the wings and fuselage there were only blackened ribs and twisted longitudinal pieces. A trail of gray smoke rose thinly until it was lost in the blue sky above the jungle.

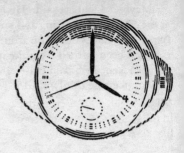

$\mathcal{T}$HE OFFICERS OF TORPEDO ELEVEN CLIMBED OUT OF THE recon cars that had brought them over to Strike Command. They wore dark glasses and some of them had on G.I. field hats with the soft brims raked down in front. There was dirt on their knees and elbows and rumps, where they had pressed against the sides or bottoms of their dugouts and foxholes.

Lambert rose as they came toward him and walked ahead of them up the side of the hill to the briefing shack. Some Marines came out of it with paint brushes and buckets. They knelt down on the top of the hill and started slapping a coat of dull green camouflage on the sides of the little building. As he passed them he heard one of them reciting a frayed verse about Noumea:

> *"The oldest place in town*
> *Is strangely called Ile Nou*
> *The temperature at midday*
> *Is a hundred and ninety-two."*

He opened the screen door and went inside the briefing room. The other Marine took up the doggerel:

> *"There is very little water*
> *And very little grass*
> *You can take New Caledonia . . ."*

Lambert walked across the cement floor and found a seat in the far corner. The others came in and took seats facing the blackboard at the front of the room. Others stopped by the table that held the big *papier-mâché* bas-relief of southern Bougainville. One of the pilots pointed to the Kahili airstrip.

"It's a grand old place," he said solemnly and walked away to his seat near the other door.

Lambert saw McRae come in with Cordell. He watched for Forsyth and finally saw him come in with four others. The officers talked and smoked and drew little sketches on the blackboard or stood around looking at the green bas-relief of Kahili.

He lighted a cigarette and leaned back in his chair. One of the junior officers passed around paper and pencils, and finally they were all seated, drumming on their chairs with their pencils. Lambert looked around the room for Babe, but he could not see him. He heard a Hudson taking off on an afternoon search and listened to it drone out over the sea. He wondered if Charlie would catch any of the patrol planes on his way back; there were generally a few float Zeros lurking off Choiseul.

Babe opened the door and came into the room. He stood with the door half-open for a moment, looking for Lambert.

"Close it. Close it," the officers shouted. "Let's keep out the flies."

Babe flushed and closed the door quickly. Lambert noticed that he looked haggard. His face was streaked with dirt, but Ben could see that he had taken time to put on a washed shirt.

Babe crossed the front of the room and sat down beside Lambert. He took off his cap and laid it over his bare knee.

"You just made it," Lambert said. "How was the trip?"

Babe wiped the sweat from his forehead. "Terrible," he said. "Christ!"

"Did you get anything?"

"Sure," Babe said. "I got everything I wanted. Even a green thigh bone for Forsyth."

"Bring back any skulls?"

"No," Babe said. "God, no. I've never seen so many skulls."

"How far'd you go?"

"Top of Kokumbona," Babe said. "I'm worn out."

"Any snipers?"

"Yes," Babe said. "Three of them. We were walking along the river and a machine gun started shooting at us."

"Anybody hurt?"

"No," Babe said. "We were just lucky. We ducked back into the underbrush. There was a big cave up on the other side of the river bank—like a Navajo cliff-dwelling. One of the Marines threw some rocks into the river ahead of us and they started shooting again from the cave. As soon as we knew where they were, the Marine lieutenant heaved up two grenades."

"Any more trouble?"

"No," Babe said. "They were dead when we climbed up. I got a flag and a Luger. Then we heard the bombs dropping here and started back."

"What were the bastards eating?"

"Rice," Babe said. "Rice and cocoanuts."

"They didn't have a searchlight, did they?"

"No," Babe said. "The others looked for a while, but I went outside the cave and sat down to rest. One of the Japs had his whole chest blown out."

"Good," Lambert said. "I hope it hurt him like hell."

"He looked awful," Babe said. "God! It almost made me sick."

The officer who was passing out paper gave some to Babe, and Lambert handed him a pencil. Then the door opened and Lieutenant-Colonel Sampson came in. He was the Staff Intelligence Officer and had got his Distinguished Flying Cross during the early days at Henderson. He was a little deaf from the pitiless bombings he had been through, but he knew the Solomons thoroughly and the torpedo officers liked him.

"At ease, gentlemen," he said, when they started to rise. He walked over to the blackboard and with a few strokes drew a rough outline of the Kahili-Buin area. He put down the chalk and faced the officers. Babe could see the worn oxidized Marine crest on the cap tucked into his belt.

"Gentlemen," he said, "as you probably know, the strike tonight will be at Kahili."

The officers had stopped talking. They leaned forward to listen or stretched back in their chairs, watching him respectfully.

"Naturally," he said, "the detailed plans will be given you tonight before you take off. I'll give you the general scheme now so that you can be thinking about it before the final briefing tonight." He cleared his throat and picked up the chalk again. He was short and well built and dark enough to be a *jai-alai* player.

"Take-off time is scheduled for a half-hour after midnight— zero-zero thirty. That should give you maximum moonlight over the harbor when you get there. The Army is sending as many heavy bombers as they can get off the field—probably about twenty. They'll bomb the defense area around the harbor and try to knock out the ack-ack and searchlight installations before you gentlemen arrive. Is that right, Captain?"

An Army captain in the back of the room stood up. "That's right, sir," he said. "The way it looks now, we'll only have about fifteen planes for you. Charlie kicked us around a little this afternoon."

The Navy fliers chuckled appreciatively.

"At any rate," Sampson said, "Charlie will be awake when you get there." He turned to the blackboard. "You'll go up the Slot as usual until you get to Bougainville Strait. We're planning on thirty-five TBFs for the strike. Twenty will carry mines; ten, torpedoes; and five, a 2,000 pounder each. All planes except the five carrying eggs will fly over Bougainville Strait and then turn west here." He made an X on the board. "You'll swing around southwest until you see the pass north of Kahili. Then, from 2,000 feet, you'll start figuring your approach to the harbor. Charlie won't be expecting you to come in from the north and the surprise should be worth a few seconds to you."

"How about the planes with eggs?" an officer asked. He sketched lazily on his notepaper.

"They'll orbit just south of Fauro," Sampson said, "for approximately eight minutes."

Babe wrote *eight minutes* and underlined the words.

"By that time Charlie should be looking for you with his searchlights." He leaned back against the table. "That's where the plunge-bombing comes in. You lads with eggs will be at 1,800 feet waiting for the searchlights. When Charlie snaps them on, *you* put them out. We don't want him to see where the mines are laid."

He turned to the board and began drawing a solid line between East Point and Moila Point. "Mines have been sown about three-quarters of the way from East to Moila," he said. "Tonight you'll finish the job."

"How much shipping is there off Buin?" an officer asked.

"One large attack-cargo ship, a small supply ship and three barges," Sampson said. "Let's get them if we can. When the mining's finished, the planes with fish can go in for a try at them."

"Why not lay the mines after?" an ensign asked.

Some of the others started to laugh, but Sampson held up his hand. "It's a good question," he said. "You junior pilots are expected to ask questions like that whenever you don't know the answers." He spoke to the ensign. "The planes that are dropping the mines have to go slower than the others," he said. "Otherwise the chutes would rip off the mines when they're dropped. It takes them a longer time to finish their job. When the torpedo planes come down, they can travel faster and there're fewer of them. They'll be exposed to fire a shorter length of time than the mine-layers would be if they had to go last."

"Thank you, sir," the ensign said. He looked defiantly at the officers who had laughed.

"When it's over," Sampson continued, "form up if you can, and fly back in formation. It'll be easier to count noses that way. If you get lost or hurt, or your compass is shot out, go up to 5,000 feet and look around for flares. Is that right, Mr. Vaughan?"

A New Zealand flight-lieutenant stood up. "Right, sir," he said. "We'll be flying the Hudson at 5,000, dropping parachute flares every five minutes. If you don't know which way to fly, just follow the flares and you'll be back for breakfast."

The pilots laughed and one of them clapped him on the back as he sat down. "Thank you, Mr. Vaughan," the Colonel smiled. "I hope you gentlemen will remember his good advice." He fumbled inside his shirt pocket and brought out a sheet of paper. He unfolded it and looked around the room. "I have the list of your strike assignments," he said. "The first twenty officers will carry mines in their bays: *Harking . . . Thompson . . . Graham . . . Cordell . . . Evans . . . Wilkinson . . . Lovering . . . Harrison . . .*" He finished the list.

"The next group will have torpedoes: *Weatherall . . . Lewis . . . Forsyth . . . Ashford . . . Soresi . . . Flynn . . . McRae . . . Shackleford . . . Hamilton . . . Gray.*"

Babe looked at the flies buzzing against the screened side of the room. Tonight he would carry a fish.

Forsyth drew a picture of a huge torpedo speeding toward a battleship that looked like a pagoda.

"Just my luck," Cordell said to Forsyth. "Want to trade?"

"No, thanks," Eliot said. "I like it fine."

Lambert put down his pencil and folded his notepaper. Plunge-bombing would be all right for a change.

"That leaves five for the eggs," Sampson said. *"Williams . . . French . . . Brown . . . Lambert . . .* and *McIntyre.*" He put the list back into his pocket and buttoned it. "If you'll come up to the map, I'll show you where everything is."

The officers got out of their chairs and crowded in a semi-circle around the bas-relief table. Babe got up and walked over behind Lambert. His feet felt swollen and waterlogged. The muscles in his legs were sore.

"Can you all see, gentlemen? Those of you in the rear can stand on chairs, if you can't." He pointed to the shore line on the map. "The shipping is anchored here—just off Jakohina Mission. There's also some ack-ack on the beach near Kangu and at the mouth of the Uguimo River. If you torpedo pilots can get through, go ahead. If there's a heavier concentration of fire than we think—forget it. We'd rather have you come back."

"How about the mining?" Lovering asked.

"You'll lay them here, roughly," Sampson said. "We'll have exact maps for you tonight."

"How about the ack-ack?" McIntyre asked. "Which spots should we try to knock out?"

"Whichever seem to be putting out the most stuff," the Colonel said. "But the emplacements on Erventa Island and Pupukuna Point should be the worst. Charlie has searchlights there, too. It's a good bet you'll knock out something."

"Which way do we come out?"

"The easiest and fastest way," Sampson said. He pointed to the map. "There's some ack-ack on Shortland, so stay to the east of it if you can. Once you're past there, you're safe."

He saw that some of them had raised their eyes and were grinning at him.

"Hell," the Colonel said, "it's just a short swim back from there."

He edged out from in front of the table and the officers closed in. When they had made their notes, they moved away and others filled in. Babe copied some of the names on his notepaper. He wanted to have the names right so that he could tell Marge about it in the letter tomorrow.

He heard Cordell beside him. "I'm going down to the planes," he said. "I'll tell your captain you want a torpedo tonight."

"Thanks," Babe said. He was glad he did not have to go down to Henderson again before the strike.

Two pilots next to him were talking. "This is a big strike," one said. "I wonder what's behind it."

"Hell," the other said. "Uncle Bull wants it. That's good enough for me."

Lambert touched the New Zealand pilot on the shoulder. "Mike," he said, "drop over to the Squadron for a drink before mess."

"Thanks, laddie. I will. I've been dry as dust for weeks."

"Here's your chance," Ben said. "Glad to have you."

"Good show this afternoon," Vaughan said.

"Yes," Ben said, "good show. Your lads did well."

"They did get a few," he said. "We lost young Gordon—a fine lad. Knew his family at Invercargill—South Island, you know."

"Yes," Ben said.

"Cheer-o, then. See you in a bit."

Lambert walked over to McRae and Forsyth, who were standing by the door, talking.

"You're a pair of lucky guys," he said. "I'm playing egg-jockey again."

"I don't know how the Colonel dreams up the assignments," Forsyth said. "He must pull our names out of a hat."

"Baloney. He lets the pros carry the fish."

"Listen to him," Forsyth said. "And I haven't got half the hours he has."

"That's a lie, and you know it," Lambert said. "You had your wings when I was still in training."

"Drink before chow?" McRae asked.

"Sure," Lambert said. "I've asked Vaughan over, too."

"Fine," Forsyth said. "I like those colorful stories of his."

"He's a nice chap," McRae said. "We've always got a drink for him."

They opened the door and stood on the hill looking at Henderson. The bomb craters had been filled and some men were laying metal mats where the old ones had been torn up by the explosions.

"I filled my foxhole like a motherless child," McRae said. "I don't like these afternoon raids."

"We'll keep Charlie awake tonight," Forsyth said. He put on his baseball cap and squinted at the orange sun over Esperance.

"My jeep's parked down below," McRae said. "I'll drive you back to the Squadron."

They walked down the side of the hill, past the sandbagged entrance, to the level ground below. As they looked back up the hill they could see the other officers filing out of the doorway and the two Marines painting camouflage on the roof.

Evening

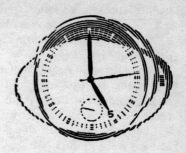

*N*INE OF THEM SAT IN McRAE'S TENT, TALKING AND DRINKING
raw Australian whiskey from the Squadron Commander's big
gallon bottle. Scott had brought along half a box of rare nickel
cigars for the others.

"They've got an ice machine at Tulagi," McRae said.
"Turns out a bushel of shaved ice an hour." He looked at his
own warm drink in the thermos top.

"They can't use that much," Forsyth said. "Maybe they'd
like to trade some of it."

"Sure they would," Lambert said. "For liquor."

"Anyway," Forsyth said, "one of us could fly the Duck over
for a bushel each afternoon."

"It sounds fine," McRae said. "But what've we got that they
want?"

"Not much, I guess," Cordell said. He felt his chin and
realized that he needed a shave again.

"What do they do for drinks over there?" Forsyth asked.
He sipped his drink slowly, letting the warm whiskey stay in
his mouth awhile before swallowing.

"Torpedo alcohol," McRae said. "From the PTs. The

119

maintenance officer's going crazy. The men steal the stuff and sell it to the officers' mess for fifty bucks a gallon."

"Do they mix it?" Vaughan, the New Zealander, asked. "Or do they like it neat?"

"They cut it, all right," McRae said. "They'd all be dead if they drank that stuff straight. It's two hundred proof. They mix it with canned orange juice or squeeze wild limes. It makes a hell of a drink with a little of that shaved ice."

"This is bloody good," Vaughan said. "Our blokes haven't had any come in for a fortnight."

"One of us better get some leave," McRae said. "The bottle won't last forever."

"My oath it won't," Vaughan said. "Not if you're always inviting stray dogs like myself for a drink."

"That's what it's for," McRae said. "Let me freshen yours."

"Not for the moment, please," Vaughan said. "I'm doing rather nicely."

"The chlorine in the water does something to it," Cordell said. "Makes it taste damned strange."

"Good, I'd say," Scott said. He stood up and passed around the cigars. "Take some back with you, Mr. Vaughan," he said.

"Thanks so much," Vaughan said. He took two, put one in his pocket and unwrapped the other. "By God, your American cigars *are* good. Fair dinkum."

The others laughed and McRae took a cigar from Scott.

"We've got plenty of spare torpedo juice," Cordell said.

"Forget about it," McRae growled. "It may be expendable, but I still have to account for it."

"Put it down to *Recreation and Morale*," Lambert said. He poured some whiskey into his metal cup and cut it with canteen water.

"Were you on the Hudson that bellied-in this morning?" Scott asked.

"No," Vaughan said. "Some other blokes."

"Were they badly hurt?"

"Not very. Cracked skull and a broken collar bone. They'll be flown down to Wellington tomorrow."

"Any chance of your going?"

"Not much," Vaughan said. "I've only been here four months. Maybe I'll go back in another three."

"How long's it been since you were home?" Cordell asked.

"Only about a year," Vaughan said. "They kept me instructing the young lads for a time."

"What were you doing before the war?" Scott asked.

"Flying," Vaughan said. "I was with our National Airways."

"What'd you fly?" McRae asked.

"The old De Havilands and Sikorsky flying boats. Whatever we had."

"What route did you have?" Lambert asked.

Vaughan smiled. "All of them at one time or another—Dutch East Indies, Auckland to Sydney. Fiji, Samoa, Singapore, Hong Kong, Manila—most of the Pacific."

"An Old China Hand," Lambert said.

Vaughan grinned. "A *burra sahib*," he said.

"What's that one?" Forsyth asked. "I know what *pukka sahib* means. What's *burra*?"

"Very top-drawer," Vaughan said. "*Pukka-pukka.*"

"Is your wife from New Zealand?" Cordell asked. He poured himself another drink.

"No," Vaughan said. "She's English. I met her in Hong Kong and married her in Bombay. Her father was an Army Colonel—very *pukka*, y'know. I used to be home a few days every month before the war, but not any more. They wouldn't let me join the Air Force until Japan came into it. Then the Nips swallowed up everything and there bloody well wasn't any place left to fly to, so they let me join." He put down his cup and ran his hand through his thick black hair. "I liked it at that," he said. "It was a good life."

"I always wanted to go to those places," Forsyth said. "I only got as far as Europe."

"I've never been to England," Vaughan said. "Perhaps that makes it even." He leaned back on the cot, enjoying the cigar.

"What were those places like?" Forsyth asked. "Singapore and Hong Kong?"

"I had a home at Singapore," Vaughan said, "and Judy's brother always had an Army crowd at the house. In those days everybody dressed for dinner and drank a lot to forget the war we knew was coming."

"Did you know it, then, Keith?" McRae asked.

"I think so," Vaughan said. "Most of us felt we couldn't always have those things and so we enjoyed them while we could. But . . . I made Judy go back to Invercargill. The rest of them . . ." he shrugged his shoulders, ". . . are dead or dying, I suppose. There'll never be anything like it again. Even when they knew everything was gone, they didn't leave. Our friends and their children, the servants—they didn't leave." He slapped at a mosquito on his thigh. "First wog today," he said. "Your screen doors are very good, aren't they?"

"We're lucky to have them," McRae said. "I had to bully some Seabees to have them made."

"May I have a spot more?"

"Of course."

Vaughan went over to the table and tilted the big bottle. "This *is* a whopper," he said. "We don't have them like that."

"Neither do we, really," McRae said. "That's a display bottle—for advertising."

"Oh, yes," Vaughan said. "It must be very effective." He went back to the cot.

"Did you see the fun this afternoon?" Scott asked.

"Yes. Quite a bash, wasn't it? How many Nips did you get?"

"About thirty," Scott said. "Hendricks, there, got two."

"Wack-o," Vaughan said. "Here's to you, leftenant."

"Thanks," the young Marine said. "No trouble at all."

"What did you bag?"

"A Zero and a Mitsubishi."

"You didn't dogfight?"

"No," Hendricks said. He sat up on McRae's sea chest and leaned forward to pour himself another drink from the bottle. "I saw what happened to George Horner. . . . I saw him die in his chute."

"Nasty," Vaughan said. "My bloody oath it was."

"They had a tent together," Scott explained.

"Yeah," Hendricks said. "I'm bad news as a roommate. I'll get his things together tonight."

"It's no fun when your cobbers are killed," Vaughan said. "I know."

"Where were you when the Japs attacked?" Lambert asked. He lighted a cigarette and put the match in an ash tray made from a Jap mess kit.

"At Singapore," Vaughan said. "They told me to fly out while I could, so I loaded the old plane with everything she'd take and came out. I bloody well never thought she'd get off the water."

"How'd you get back?"

Vaughan smiled a little. "There wasn't much choice by then," he said. "I got over to Batavia and then Koepang. Oddly enough, the next stop was here at Choiseul. . . . Then down to Noumea and Auckland. We flew nights and slept days. . . . The women got a bit restless. No decent food for them, y'know."

One of the Navy fighter pilots spoke up. "Did you go into the R.N.Z.A.F. then?"

"Yes," Vaughan said. "They finally let me in. Wouldn't give me combat, like you youngsters, though. Put a sextant in my hand and told me to teach navigation."

"How the hell old are you?" McRae asked.

"Thirty-two," Vaughan said.

"The hell you are! You don't look it, but I'll bet you're five years over that."

Vaughan's eyes twinkled. "Cheer-o," he said. "I'm getting no younger." He drank from his cup and when he looked at McRae again their eyes met.

"My lad'll be in soon," he said. "Learning his navigation now."

"Will you be sorry to see him in?" Forsyth asked.

"I think not. It's hard to say. He wants to do it." Vaughan knocked the ash from his cigar very carefully into the tray. "Are all you chaps on the strike tonight?"

"All except the fighter boys," Scott said, "and me. I keep the home fires burning."

"Have they got a strike for us tomorrow?" one of the fighter pilots asked.

"Don't think so," Hendricks said. "They'll probably find something by noon."

"I'd like to get another look at Rekata."

"Float Zeros," Hendricks said. "You always think you'll catch one on the water."

"Some day I will," the other pilot said. "I hope we go to Rekata."

"Watch out for Kawanishis," the third pilot said, and they all laughed. The big four-engined flying boats were as large as the old Sikorsky clippers and very clumsy.

"We've got to get over to our mess," Hendricks said. The three fighter pilots stood up, finishing their drinks.

"You can eat with us if you like," McRae said, "but maybe your chow is just as bad."

"It's probably worse," Hendricks said. "Thanks a lot for the drinks. I'll let you know when our bootlegger makes a delivery."

They put their tin cups on the table and went out of the tent. The others listened until they heard the jeep drive out to the road.

"I must be getting back, too," Vaughan said.

"Oh, no," McRae said, "you're staying with us."

"You're very kind," Vaughan said. "But I'm responsible for the tripe that's served up at our place. If I'm not there to take the blame, the lads will feel cheated."

"I'll drive you back, then," Lambert said. He got up and put his empty cup on the table beside the bottle.

"Good-o," Vaughan said. "I'll be much obliged."

Cordell poured some whiskey into his cup.

"Will you come to the movies later?" McRae asked. "There's plenty of room. Just bring your own netting."

Vaughan laughed. "No, thank you," he said. "The wogs will get quite enough of me at my own digs. I've got to write the missis and the lad. I always do before a strike."

"So do I," Cordell said. "You never know."

"Okay?" Lambert asked.

"Right-o," Vaughan said. "Thanks again for the cigars, and my oath, gentlemen, the whiskey was fine."

"It was terrible," McRae said. "We're glad you were good enough to help us finish it."

Lambert walked out of the tent, down the board walk to the jeep, and Vaughan followed him.

"What's your job tonight?" Vaughan asked.

"A one-ton egg," Lambert said. They got in the jeep and Lambert backed around to the road. The trucks were not using it now and they drove along at thirty, glad that there was so little dust.

It was cooler now that the sun was going down, and away from Henderson, the evening seemed very quiet. Beside the road, under some palms, there was a large bomb-dispersal area. Cattle were grazing among the bombs, and a little goat ran up to the top of a pile of thousand-pounders, watching the jeep drive by. An ordnance crew was loading a one-ton bomb on a carrier.

"Those your blokes?" Vaughan asked.

"Yes," Lambert said. "Maybe my bomb, too."

"Good luck to you, lad," Vaughan said. "I wish I could do a bit more."

"Forget it," Lambert said. "Nobody'd go if you weren't along to get us back."

"Rot," Vaughan said. "We're just in the way."

"Each time I start back," Lambert said, "the first thing I look for is those flares. Hell, I can't navigate at night."

They drove past an aluminum salvage pile that would be sent back to the States. It was about fifty feet high, and on it were the crushed bodies and wings of Zeros, Kites, P-39s, Wildcats and SBDs.

"It'll be bigger tomorrow," Vaughan said. "We're contributing this morning's Hudson."

"There'll be some from this afternoon, too," Lambert said.

"Watch that you don't end up there, lad."

"All of us try not to," Lambert said. "Nobody wants to crack up."

The shadows of the palms lay across the road, and the only noise they could hear was the low purr of the exhaust. They went by one of the bivouac areas and saw a line of men standing by the mess kitchen. They had their mess gear, and near them two blackened oil drums steamed over a wood fire. From the jeep they could hear the men talking and the rattling of their mess kits.

The road turned up past Fighter Two and an engine coughed harshly as they went by. A bomb-carrier came down the road toward them, jolting ponderously and, as they passed, Lambert squinted a little and drove through the veil of dust that hung suspended in the still evening air.

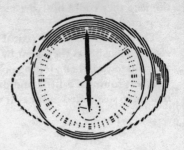

*B*ABE CAME INSIDE THE TENT CARRYING HIS CLOTHES THAT HAD dried on the line. They were stiff and wrinkled and he hoped that the soap had been rinsed out. He folded the shirt and a pair of shorts and put them in his flight bag. Then he closed the bag again and sat on his cot looking at the things from Kokumbona on the table. His old flight suit lay across the cot, its legs wet up to the knees, where he had waded through the Matanikau. He hung it on the nail behind his cot and sat down again, feeling better than he had when he went up for the briefing. The nap had done him good. His leg muscles were not as sore as they had been.

He could hear Forsyth singing as he walked toward the tent:

> ". . . I've got tuppence to spend
>   and tuppence to lend
> And tuppence to send home to my wife."

Babe wondered how long Marge would keep getting his allotment if he did not come back from the strike.

> ". . . I've got nopence
>   Jolly, jolly nopence
> I've got nopence
>   To last me all my life . . ."

Babe went over to the door and saw Eliot coming toward the tent. He wished that he had gone over for a drink with him. Hell, he needed the rest more than the drink. He'd go over tomorrow before dinner.

> ". . . Happy is the day
>   When the airman gets his pay
> As we go rolling, rolling home."

"How was the party?" Babe asked.

"Fine," Eliot said. "Swell. Grand—or should it be Garand?"

"Was the new pilot there?" Babe asked.

"No," Eliot said. "We'll ask him before he goes on his first strike." He came into the tent and threw his cap and gloves down on his cot. "The maid service at this hotel stinks. Next week they'll have white and blue signs saying *Please Conserve Hot Water* and *The Supply of Towels Is Limited*." He went out of the tent and Babe could hear him filling the wash helmet from the big can.

"I brought a bone for you," Babe called.

"Good," Eliot said, sloshing water over his face. "I'll put it out in the sun tomorrow." He dried his face and hands and came back into the tent for his cap.

"Ready for chow?"

"I guess so," Babe said. He did not feel hungry, but he knew that if he did not eat he would tire more quickly on the way back from Kahili.

"I don't give a damn for food any more," Eliot said, as they walked down the path. "I'm just eating out of habit. Tonight

129

we'll have bully beef—cold or fried or roasted or covered with stale bread crumbs—or it'll be that damned luncheon meat cooked the same way."

"I don't mind luncheon meat," Babe said.

"Wait'll you've been here a few months. You'll be sick of it then."

"Marge says meat is rationed back home."

"Why?" Eliot asked. "So the boys on Guadal can have filets? Hell, no! Because farmers won't kill their cattle. The guys doing the fighting aren't getting it. I never ate less in my life."

"Maybe they can't get it out to us."

"Why not? They've had long enough to get things moving our way. What the hell's the Navy for?"

They saw the others going into the shadowed mess hall ahead of them. Now that the sun was going down, the building looked darker and they could hear the clatter of plates and the high-pitched cackling of mess attendants in the galley. Babe wondered if his uncle was holding out for better cattle prices. He would write him tomorrow and tell him how long it had been since he had eaten a steak.

There was a plate of cold corned beef on their table and a pile of crackers beside it. Forsyth sat down and reached for the bowl of rice.

"Have some rice," he said. "It's the only thing warm."

"I'll try a little," Babe said, dipping a spoon into the bowl. He put a piece of butter on the mound of rice and waited for it to melt.

Forsyth took some of the shredded red meat from the platter and passed it to Babe. "I guess they've run out of ways to disguise it," he said. "This way it's the least disagreeable." He took a cracker and buttered it.

Babe saw that the butter on his rice was not melting.

Forsyth looked at him. "Forget about that wax," he said.

"Melting point's too high. The rice'd have to be steaming to soften it."

They saw Lambert come into the mess hall. He walked to their table and sat down beside Babe. "It's a nice evening," he said. "Hope the weather stays this way all night."

"When's the final briefing?"

"Midnight," Lambert said. "We're getting the pre-game rally at twenty-four hundred on top of picturesque Pagoda Hill." He filled his plate with rice and meat and reached for the plate of crackers. "Any water?" he asked.

Forsyth flagged down a mess boy and held up his metal cup wordlessly. The boy ambled off toward the galley.

"Where's Junior?" Lambert asked. "I haven't seen him lately."

"When last seen, the flag secretary was diving for a foxhole—gas mask in one hand and *aiguillette* in the other."

"Has he crawled out yet?"

"Probably just now—in time to hold the Admiral's chair," Forsyth said. "We mustn't forget the amenities."

The mess boy came back and filled the water cups.

"Any tea this evening?" Lambert asked.

"No, suh. Jus' coffee."

"You can bring it any time."

Babe moved his fork around the plate, mixing the rice with the cold meat.

"Where's your appetite?" Forsyth asked. "You should be hungry after your trip."

"I guess I'm just nervous," Babe said. "I'll eat something before we take off." He passed the atabrine to one of the other pilots.

"Did Vaughan have any hot dope?"

"No," Lambert said. "His bunch hears even less than we do."

"Going to the movies?"

"Not planning to. I've seen it."

"I think I'll go," Babe said. "I need some laughs."

"We all do, kid," Lambert said. He drank the water in his cup and refilled it with hot coffee. He began to sip it and heard a Cat splutter over the trees as it took off. He listened for a moment and put down his cup. "The P-boat must be going up for Barnes," he said.

Forsyth looked at his watch. "Yes," he said, "that would be it."

"Maybe he'll be back for breakfast," Babe said. Each time a pilot was rescued, it gave him more confidence. Soon, he thought, he would be like the others and not worry about being shot down and living with natives while waiting to be rescued.

"Weather must be good up the Slot," Lambert said. He wondered if they would ever have to send up a Cat after him.

Forsyth pushed aside his plate and took out a cigarette. He offered the package to Lambert.

"No, thanks," Lambert said. "Coffee first."

"You've got an iron stomach," Forsyth said.

"No," Ben said. "I just want to get the taste of that rice out of my mouth."

An SBD pilot came over to the table and spoke to Lambert. "How about some poker tonight, Ben?" he asked. "The boys want revenge."

"Sounds good," Ben said. "What time?"

"Whenever you feel like it. Just drop over. You're flying on the strike, so we'll knock off early. I'll tell the boys to start warming up the cards."

As he walked away they heard the door open and saw an ensign come in with the mail.

"Here it is," Forsyth said. "And I'll settle for just one V-Mail letter. You're due for plenty, Babe."

Babe watched the other officers crowding around the table, while the ensign sorted the letters and packages into little piles.

"Forsyth," somebody called. "Come and get it."

Eliot grinned and got up from the table. He walked over to the officers and a letter was passed back to him. He looked at the writing and came back to his seat.

"Cheer up," Lambert said. "Who's it from—your sister?"

"No," Forsyth said. "Not as bad as that. It's from Mother."

"Good enough," Ben said. He finished his coffee. "I'll take that smoke now."

Eliot gave him the package and struck a light for him.

"What would you do if all this ended tomorrow?" Ben asked.

"You mean the war?"

"Yes," Ben said. "Where would you go?"

"Home, of course. Then I'd get out my boat and sail for a month. A whole month without anybody else. Just a galley full of steaks and frozen vegetables and no war to fight. Fish when I want to, sleep or race with the gulls. Maybe I could find myself again that way."

"I hope you will," Ben said.

"I don't want to think that far ahead until it's over, though."

"I know how you feel," Ben said. "If it ends, I'll think about it then."

Babe left them for the crowd around the mail table.

"I hope he gets one," Forsyth said.

"Yes," Ben said. "It must mean a lot to him." He looked out of the side and saw that it was growing dark. The sun had gone down behind the jungle, leaving the gray of evening.

"Why is it," Forsyth asked, "that they try to fight every war with slogans? You know: 'Make the World Safe' . . . and all of that bilge?"

"It's for the morons," Ben said. "If we could get all of the broadcasts from the States, I'll bet we'd hear more slogans than there are fighting men."

"The Four Freedoms," Forsyth said. "What the hell does that mean to you?"

"To me?" Lambert asked. "Nothing."

"That's the way I feel about it," Forsyth said. "I have an idea why I'm out here, but it's not because of any slogan. It always seems that the guys who are the busiest with the war have the least to say about it. They can't even complain when somebody frames a set of phrases for them to die for."

"I don't like it either," Lambert said. "I never cared much for mottoes."

Babe came back with three letters, grinning self-consciously.

"Anybody else get any?" Forsyth asked.

"Yeah. The skipper and Joe Cordell. They picked them up."

Lambert shrugged his shoulders. "Run along and read them," he said. "I'll see you over at Pagoda Hill."

"At midnight," Babe said.

"Right."

They watched Babe turn away and start to open one of the letters. He began to read it in the dim light of the mess hall and then folded it and put on his cap as he went out the door.

There were a few scattered letters left on the table as they passed it. A mess attendant stood at the door beside a big cardboard box of cigarettes. He handed a carton to Eliot and one to Ben as they went out of the mess hall together.

It was getting cool outside, and walking over to their quarters they slapped at mosquitoes and talked quietly while the red glow of their cigarettes traced little scallops in the darkness about them.

Night

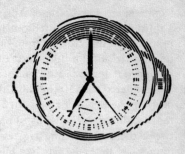

$\mathcal{T}$HE SQUADRON COMMANDER GOT UP FROM HIS SOLITAIRE GAME and clicked on his radio. Having lost seven dollars to himself, he turned the dials of the short-wave receiver irritably. He listened to the static for a moment and then turned it off. It was the only radio in the squadron and sometimes the others came in and listened to it during the afternoons.

McRae went back to the table and gathered together the worn cards. They felt damp and greasy as he shuffled them and he told himself that he would ask the next officer who went on leave to bring him back a few decks. Beyond the cone of light thrown by the single bulb, the tent was dark. He looked upward and watched the insects that the light had attracted. They circled in and out of the shadows below the cardboard shade, and he squinted his eyes for a moment and pretended that the little insects were planes caught at the apex of a battery of searchlights. Then the glare hurt him and he turned away.

He drummed the pack of cards nervously on the table top and then put it down and went over to the shelf above his sea chest. He felt for one of the metal cups and brought it back to the table. The bottle of Australian whiskey was less than a third full, but he poured out half a cup. He held the cup in his fingers and tilted it from side to side, watching the dark liquid swirl until a little vortex formed in the center. Then he sipped it appreciatively and set the cup down on the table. He wondered what it would be like to be back in a night club far from the war, drinking with other people in a well-lighted room with waiters and a band playing and a girl walking between the tables selling cigarettes. He would order a big dinner—whatever he felt like having—and then sit back and watch the floor show. Maybe he'd have a girl, but there'd be one later at any rate.. They'd go up to his suite and there'd be a big bottle of champagne sweating in the ice bucket and he'd take it out and hold it with a white starched napkin and pull the cork slowly and then it would pop and the cold golden bubbles would come pouring out in a torrent and he'd fill the long-stemmed glasses and sit beside her and sip the chilled wine and light her cigarette and tell her how long it was since he had been close to a woman.

He had almost forgotten what it was like to hear music or to dance with a girl in an evening dress who wore orchids at her shoulder. He drank from the cup again and twirled it in his fingers before he put it down. He leaned back in his chair and looked up at the top of the tent. It was so dark that he could barely see the top and he looked at it for a minute and then leaned forward, feeling the rustle of the letter in his pocket. He unbuttoned the flap and felt that the button was coming loose. He took out the envelope and unfolded the letter. It had been written on a single sheet of blue stationery by a woman who was the widow of one of his classmates. He held the letter directly under the light and read it again.

Larry, my dear:

It was wonderful to get your letter of sympathy so soon after we knew that Frank had been lost. The first shock has left me and I search the remnants of my life, looking for the things and the people I'll always want to remember.

You must know that you are one of those people and that I want desperately to recover a little of what I have lost and neglected.

I think of you so often and pray that you may come back from the hell around you. If you should be killed I think that there would be little I could live for. Please be careful of yourself.

I shall live here for a little while until I decide what I must do. I've got to see you when you come back, Larry. Don't fail me.

My gratitude and my love.

                                                        Miriam

Don't fail me, he thought, and you failed me when I needed you most. He sipped slowly from the cup again and put down the letter on the table. It lay still and unresisting before him—an instrument of confession that had opened the thoughts of years gone by, of lives he had never lived. He had thought it was over, but the thing that he had wanted so many times had come again and he knew that now the choice was his, the way it had once been hers. The open letter lay on the rough table top and the shadows of insects under the light darted across it.

He looked at the darkness on the other side of the tent and then got up slowly and went over to the radio. The yellow light of the dial snapped on and he held the volume low until he could hear a voice over the static. He looked at the frequency and saw that it was Radio Tokyo. He knelt beside the set, listening to the tinny jazz that blared out, and when the piece had ended in a flurry of drum beats, the announcer spoke: For the enlightenment of the misinformed Americans, the Imperial Japanese Navy had scored another crushing victory over the shattered fleet of the criminal Roosevelt. Five battleships, eight cruisers and sixteen destroyers had been sunk yesterday. The Americans must see by now that it was useless to try to interfere longer with the consolidation of East Asia into an economically independent sphere. And now some letters from Australian prisoners of war would be read. They were all well treated and in good health and anxious to have Australia drop out of the war so that they could return to their neglected homes. The announcer read five letters and said that this was a courtesy of the Tokyo Broadcasting Corporation and that, as a special feature, letters from prisoners of war would be broadcast each night at this time. The radio was silent for a moment and then he could hear the strains of *"There's a Long Long Trail a-Winding"* fighting through the static.

McRae listened to a few bars and then turned it off. He went back to the table and finished his drink, holding up the cup so that the last drops reached his tongue. Then he walked over and put the cup back on the shelf.

Somebody knocked at his screen door and he came back to the table and stood in front of the light.

"Come in," he said.

"Good evening, Commander." It was his plane captain.

"Hello, Thompson," he said. "Everything set?"

"Yes, sir," Thompson said, closing the door behind him. "The plane is bombed-up and your engine sounds sweet."

"Good. How about the others?"

"Most of them are loaded. The ones that aren't will be ready in a half hour."

"How's the radio?"

"Perfect. Lawson's been with me gettin' her checked over."

"In a hurry?"

"No, sir. Not particularly."

"Sit down, then. Take it easy. You look worn out."

"I am pretty tired, sir. I been workin' on her since you brought her back from Russell." He sat down on the edge of McRae's cot.

"Care for a drink?" McRae pointed to the bottle.

"I sure would, sir. It'd be mighty good."

McRae brought a cup from the shelf and poured a shot into it from the bottle.

"You having one, sir?"

"No," McRae said, handing the cup to him. "I've had mine for tonight."

"This makes the second since we left Pearl, sir. Here's luck to you."

"To all of us," McRae said.

"Right, sir." He tasted it tentatively and then took a good swallow.

"Want a chaser?"

"Not on your life," Thompson said, smiling. "I been dreamin' about a drink for so long I don't want to spoil it."

"I wish there was enough for everybody," McRae said.

"I hear they're going to start gettin' some beer on this island," Thompson said. "Do you know whether there's any truth in it?"

"I don't know," McRae said. "But they ought to be getting something out here for the men."

"Any chance of us gettin' relieved, sir?"

"Sure," McRae said. "There's always that chance."

"Seems like we've been here an awful long time."

"Yes," McRae said. "It does seem that way."

Thompson raised the cup to his lips and swallowed again.

"This is damn good, sir," he said. "I certainly appreciate this."

"Drink up and have another."

"No, thanks, sir. I'd like to, but I wouldn't know what to do with another. I guess I'll have to take it easy when we get back."

"Yeah," McRae said. "We'll all be a bunch of two-drink Johnnies." He sat at the table, his head beyond the light, watching the Chief enjoying his drink. It was a hell of a note that the men couldn't get any.

"How's your ear infection, sir?"

"Coming along," McRae said. "The Doc wants to take a look tomorrow."

"That's a nice-lookin' belt you got on, sir."

McRae looked down at his belt and let his fingers run across it. "Yes," he said. "I got it in Texas."

"I heard you used to be a test pilot, sir."

"After I got out of the Navy," he said, "I worked for Curtiss for a while."

"I guess you got good pay."

"Yes," McRae said. "It was good pay, all right."

"Would you rather be doing that now?"

"No. I don't think so."

"I want to get a job afterward at an aircraft factory," Thompson said, "settle down and find a wife."

"You'll have all those things coming to you," McRae said. "Make sure you get them."

"Will we get anything out of Japan, sir?"

"Like what?" McRae asked.

"I don't know. Maybe a Jap to cook for me or keep house for my wife."

"It's an idea," McRae said. "But I'd rather kill them all."

"We wouldn't never be allowed to do that, sir."

"No," McRae said. "The voters don't mind if we kill Jap soldiers or fliers, but they'll be against our doing away with the things that bred them."

Thompson put the empty cup on the table top. "Sometimes I can't figure them out back home," he said. "I guess they don't know what it's like."

"No," McRae said. "They don't know now and they never will, because by the time we get back the war'll be over and we'll be sick of talking about it and thinking about it. Anyway, they wouldn't believe us."

They sat for a moment without saying anything and then Thompson got up.

"I'd better be gettin' back, sir," he said. "What time do you want me at the plane?"

"Midnight," McRae said. "Take-off's at twelve-thirty. I'm going to turn in pretty soon."

"Thanks a lot for the drink, sir," the Chief said. "I'll catch a little sleep and have the plane ready when you come down from Pagoda."

"Fine," McRae said. "See you later."

Thompson opened the door and went out. McRae watched the beam of his flashlight bouncing from the palm trunks to the ground, lighting his way out to the road.

He put Thompson's cup back on the shelf and sat down at the table again. In the distance the engines of a B-17 turned over and fired into life. He could hear the steady roar through the cool night air. He ran his hand along the tooled leather belt he had bought in Texas. That had been on the trip back from San Diego. He had flown an SBC-3 out to the coast and the landing gear had stuck when he came in. He remembered bellying-in on the concrete and his head hitting the panel and the ambulance next to the plane and the men lifting him out of the cockpit and the wire he had sent back to the plant. Coming back by train he had gotten off at a station stop and bought the belt, because he had never seen one like it before. His wife had not liked it because she thought it was too flashy, but it was good thick leather and had lasted a long time out here, where most leather grew moldy and fell apart. He would give it to Thompson before he went back.

A bug flew against the side of his head and he put his hand up quickly but it had gone. He realized how long his hair was getting. It seemed to grow twice as fast out here. If he thought of it tomorrow he'd have one of the ordnance men cut it—good and short this time.

He wondered if Cordell would come over for cribbage. Probably not tonight—he'd be writing letters to his family, telling his kid he'd be seeing him soon and to be good to his mother now that he was the man of the house.

McRae looked at the letter lying on the table and reached over for his pipe. He filled it carefully, pressing the grains tightly so that he would lose none of them. Then he lighted it and puffed quickly at first until it was burning well. He leaned back and thought about Miriam's letter. He started to reach for it and then got up and walked over to his sea chest. He raised the top of it and saw the termite dust slide off onto the floor. He felt inside among his uniforms and skivvies until he found the box he was searching for.

Walking back to the table he heard the roar of the bomber's engines die away into the stillness of the night and he put the box of stationery in front of him and took out his fountain pen and a sheet of paper and an envelope. He addressed the envelope first and printed FREE across the upper right-hand corner.

McRae sat under the yellow cone of light for a long time while the little insects ticked against the shade above him. Then he smoothed the sheet of paper against the top of the table and began to write.

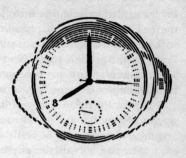

CORDELL HAD BEEN TYPING A LETTER ON HIS BATTERED portable. He pulled it out of the roll and looked at it, wishing that he could tell his wife more of the things he had done and what his life was really like, but there was no sense in having the letter cut up by the censors. It would only worry her. He read it again under the dim light of the big flashlight hanging just above his head.

My darling:

Things have been pretty much the same since I wrote you last. The mail service seems to be improving a little. I got your letter this evening at mess and it took twelve days to get to me. The V-Mail letters are okay but they're so small that it's hard to read them.

We didn't fly last night but we're going up to Kahili to-night and finish the job we started. I think we may get leave soon and, of course, it's possible that the squadron may be relieved. If we get sent back, I'll put in for instructing duty at Corpus Christi or Jacksonville. It's been so long since we've been together that I think we deserve some time for ourselves.

I'm glad to hear that little Joe is doing so well at school. It's hard to believe that he's finishing second grade. I hope he has a good vacation this summer and that maybe you'll be able to go away somewhere for a rest.

I haven't heard anything more about my promotion, but we'd be the last ones to hear about any new selection lists. Anyway, I'm due for the next half-stripe in a few weeks and the promotion will be retroactive including the extra pay and allowances. I'll be really glad to get it.

We had a big raid this afternoon but they didn't do much damage. I got into the dugout as soon as I heard Condition Red so I didn't see much of what was happening. We shot down a lot of planes and I guess it'll be a long time before Charlie tries it again.

Give my love to your mother and tell her I'll be back soon for one of her roast turkeys. Give little Joe a hug for me and tell him not to forget his dad.

All of my love to you, my dearest—

Your husband

He signed it *Joe* with a pencil stub and folded the letter in thirds. He stood up and brought out his money belt from around his waist, pulled the zipper and fingered inside the belt for his packet of air-mail stamps. He took out one and closed the belt again. Then he tucked in his shirt tails and sat down at the table. He put the stamp on the envelope and then slipped the folded letter inside and sealed the sticky flap, wondering whether he should have told her about the chill the other night. No. It would just worry her.

Cordell balanced the letter on the back of his hand and thought about it getting to her in two weeks. Cargo planes came in with mail and flew out again loaded with sacks full of letters, but he flew out with bombs or mines or torpedoes and came back with an empty bomb bay. She had never written a letter to him that complained about anything. She just told him what her life was like now that he was gone and how much she missed him and the things that little Joe did every day and how much bigger he was getting. He had seen guys get letters from their wives griping about everything—why couldn't the war stop or why didn't the Navy let him come home and why didn't the others do a little fighting—until after a while when the mail came they gritted their teeth and put the letters aside for a few days until they could face them. In all their married life she had never nagged him. It had been a crazy life, too, living on shore stations while he was with the fleet and then moving to Pensacola while he got his wings and little Joe being born at the Navy Hospital and the orders to Norfolk for carrier training and as soon as she was well enough she had followed him up the coast and found a place for them to live again. Formulas and diaper services, and a different doctor in every new place they went if there wasn't a child specialist at the Navy hospital. It had been a hell of a life for a girl, and now that she was a woman he was away and she had all of the responsibility again. There was only the chain of letters between them and the memories of her and the times when they had been with each other. He knew that she would probably not go away anywhere during the summer, but would put the money aside until he got back, hoping he'd have leave and they could go somewhere together.

He turned his hand until the letter fell off like the wing of a plane. He pushed it toward the end of the table and looked at the worn keys of his typewriter, wondering how it had held out this long in the tropics. During the rainy season it was always wet and gummy, but now that the air was dry it worked a lot better. When he came out again he'd bring one of those new Swiss machines made out of aluminum that didn't weigh more than a pair of shoes. Next time he'd know what to bring and what to leave behind. He was lucky that he'd been able to get anything at all off the *Wasp*. Almost everything that he'd had with him since he left the Academy had gone down. He'd written his wife for a new picture of her and little Joe, but it was probably coming by ship, the way half of the air mail came.

Cordell wondered if McRae would like to play cribbage for a while. Probably not. Larry would be sleeping now or checking reports from the plane captains. Lambert was away playing poker and wouldn't be back until late. He thought of writing a letter to his son, but decided against it. He'd write it tomorrow, when there wasn't so much on his mind.

He watched the bugs darting around the light. It reminded him of the way the moths and crickets used to cluster on the globe of the street lamps when he walked back from the mill in the summertime when he was a kid. He'd have his empty lunch box in one hand and his greasy coat in the other and he'd get off the bus at the corner and walk down the five dark blocks to his house, hearing the low voices of the people who were talking on their front porches. Every summer that he was in high school he had worked and made enough money so that he didn't have to ask his father for any during the winter. The men he had worked with were big tough Hunkies and Polaks who could work in the pickling house all day, bending sheet steel with their sledge hammers, and then go out and drink all night. The first time he had gotten drunk they had taken him down the line with them, buying a drink at every bar and finally ending up at a hotel in Cleveland on Sunday afternoon. He wondered if the same men were working at the mill, turning out steel for the Navy, and he thought of their crude jokes and their brutality and their willingness to do anything when it came to work and the way they chipped in for a guy's family if he'd been hurt. Yes, they'd still be there, sweating and fighting and keeping the steel moving and shouting at the craneman if he came too close.

Cordell remembered loading boxcars one morning when he was standing with his back against the side of the gondola, motioning the lift of sheet steel toward him. The crane had swung it slowly, a few inches above the floor of the car, and when he motioned the craneman to set it down, the lift kept on coming and he had waved again and, finally, when he knew that it would not stop, he vaulted over the side of the car and heard the four tons of sheet steel crunch into the wooden side of the car. He had stood beside the track, feeling sick and shaking a little and the foreman saw him and called down the craneman and found out that he had been drinking on the job. He remembered feeling the same way when another plane almost smashed into him at Pensacola. So far he had been lucky.

He began to feel a little cold and got up and went over to his sea chest and dug around until he found his light summer flying jacket. He put it on and went back to the table, listening to the sound of his feet on the floorboards of the tent. You did not notice sounds like that during the daytime because there was always the sound of planes at Henderson and the noise of jeeps and trucks on the road and the voices of men talking in the areaway. It was only at night that you could hear the sound of your shoes on wood, or a match rasping against the side of the box, or the wind rustling the leaves of the palms and the sounds of the jungle in the distance.

As he sat down, the dog tag on his chest tinkled against his St. Christopher's medal. He pulled it out of his shirt and looked at it. The dog tag was corroded with salt water and the lettering was green. The St. Christopher's medal was tarnished with his sweat. He held it up to the light and looked at it closely. *St. Christopher be my guide,* it said around the rim. He dropped it inside the vee of his shirt and the cold metal struck his chest lightly.

Wearing the jacket, he felt a little warmer, and he thought about the early spring afternoon on the Severn when the cat-boat had gone over and the three of them had held on to it for almost an hour, until one of the sub-chasers came out to get them. The water had been bitterly cold and the wind had driven it up around them so that they were wet and shivering when they climbed up the side of the little yard craft. At sick bay they had given him a shot of brandy and he remembered how much better it made him feel right away and then the hot shower when he went up to his room in Bancroft and being kidded about being a lubber and going to bed after a while and thinking that it was good to be there where it was safe and warm, watching Ted bone up for Ordnance in the morning, but you knew it might have ended another way and tried not to think about it, and after a while you turned away from the light and went to sleep.

He was feeling colder in spite of the jacket, and he put his typewriter back into its frayed case and carried it over by the sea chest. His knees felt weak as he walked back to the table and he sat down and took a box of matches from his pocket. He lighted the candle that stuck out of the top of Lambert's empty wine bottle and reached up and switched off the dangling flashlight. The little yellow flame of the candle flickered brightly, silhouetting him against the wall of the tent, and he made finger-shadows the way he did for little Joe when he was still a baby. Then, while he was watching the shadows form and melt, his breath began to come faster and his throat felt tight and he knew that the chill was coming. He got up from the seat and pulled his weapons belt from under the cot. He opened the first-aid case and took out the little brown bottle of atabrine. His canteen was on the table and he took two grain-and-a-half pills and swallowed them with a quick gulp of the brackish water. He felt cold all over now as he put the canteen back on the table and closed the first-aid case. Sitting on the cot he fought against the chill as it came over him, and he dropped his weapons belt under his bunk and lifted the mosquito netting. The flame from the candle spluttered and the pool of melted wax by the wick overflowed and ran down the side of the bottle.

Cordell stretched out on his cot, feeling his forehead grow hot with sweat as he listened to the drone of the mosquitoes under the netting. He lay there for a moment hoping he would not throw up, and heard the sudden patter of rats running across the floor. He remembered that the trap under the table would still be set, unless the bits of cheese had been taken by one of the rats that had been drowned last night. His legs began to shake, and he raised up and pulled the blanket over him. After the first chill passed he would get up and take another blanket from the corner. When the shivering really came, the one over him now would feel like a sheet.

There was no sound inside the tent for a while and then he heard a splash under the table and the frantic scratching of the rat's claws against the smooth side of the helmet. His teeth began to chatter and he drew the blanket closely around his neck to keep in as much body heat as possible. Then he began to tremble from his ankles to his shoulders. He held his feet together and tried to stop the chill, but it increased until he could hear the cot creaking. He clasped his hands, holding them tightly so that his arms would not shake so hard. The hot, rancid perspiration began to come from his pores and it rolled down the side of his face and came from his neck and his back and his chest and his loins, but the chill was reaching deeper and he felt his head begin to throb and he tensed his jaw muscles, trying to stop the chattering of his teeth, but after a while he was too tired to fight it any longer and he hugged the blanket around him closely and felt his pillow soak up the sweat from his face and neck.

When the chill stopped, he dozed off for a few minutes and then woke, feeling sick and weak. His stomach was tight, but he had not vomited. A mosquito was on his forehead and he turned wearily on the pillow to brush it off. It droned away angrily and lit again on the side of the netting near his feet. It was too dark to see, but he could hear it come to rest on the inside of the netting.

Cordell pulled the blanket down around his shoulders as the chill left him. The sweat on his face was turning cold as it evaporated, and his muscles ached from their involuntary spasms. He knew that the atabrine was working now and that it should hold him until morning. He'd have to wear all the clothes he could find tonight if he wanted to avoid another chill during the strike. It wouldn't be so bad if they didn't fly higher than eight thousand.

He sat up, letting the blanket fall to his lap, and listened for noises from the trap. Then he swung his legs around and sat on the edge of his bunk and held his head between his hands. A few drops of perspiration flowed down his fingers and he looked around at the pillow and saw the dark circle where his head had been.

He was feeling better now, but a little dizzy from the pills, and he reached over to the table and brought back the canteen. The water tasted good this time and he drank almost all of it before he screwed back the cap and put it on the table again.

The sound of a PBY racing down the dark aisle of flare-pots came through the quiet night and Cordell knew that it was one of the Black Cats taking off to send back weather dope for the strike. He lifted the mosquito netting over his head and got to his feet slowly, feeling as though he had just climbed out of a swimming pool after a race. There were several dusty blankets piled in the corner by Lambert's cot and he knelt down unsteadily in the shadows, looking for the one that was least moldy. He straightened up and unfolded a blanket and shook it a little. It smelled old and stale, like an underground cavern, but he carried it over to his cot and threw it lengthwise under the netting.

His Reising gun was leaning against the side of the tent and he picked it up and looked at it. The long .45 clip was in place and the sling hung loosely from the end of the barrel. He brought back the cocking lever and ejected a shell. It seemed to work hard, but he realized that he was still weak from the chill. He opened the zipper of his jacket, letting it hang from his shoulders. That way his shirt would have a chance to dry out. He put the Reising gun on the table next to the candle, and, sitting on the cot, he began to remove his heavy shoes. He knew the sheets must be muddy where the shoes had rubbed against them, so he left on his socks and put the shoes under the cot. He felt for his weapons belt and found the issue flashlight in its canvas holder. Ducking under the netting, he pointed the light inside and found a mosquito on his pillow. He killed it with his hand and flicked away the gray blob that remained. He looked in the corners of the netting and found another that he killed by pinching the netting.

Then he blew out the candle, and sat up on the cot with the flashlight between his legs while he tucked the netting under the mattress. When he had finished he pulled the blanket over him and turned the pillow. He snapped off the flashlight and put it under his pillow and lay in the dark, listening to the scurrying of the rats as they ran across the roof of the tent. After a while he closed his eyes and thought about walking home from his grandmother's house, watching the rain bend the trees against the summer sky. He remembered the sound of the leaves thrashing in the wind and the way the houses looked, their white fronts shining wetly in the glare from the street lights, as he walked past them in the rain a long time ago when he was a kid.

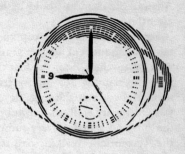

$\mathcal{E}$LIOT FORSYTH READ HIS MOTHER'S LETTER UNDER THE DIM light of the single bulb, sitting on the chair he had made out of a washed-up potato crate from Lunga Beach.

His mother and father were well, the letter said. His sister was going to have her second baby in the fall and his brother wanted to leave Andover and join the Marines. He pulled out his class pipe from his breast pocket and began filling it from a small can of cheap tobacco. He lighted the pipe and drew in, tasting the bitterness of the stem. His mother was working with the Red Cross Blood Donors' Bureau and his father was on a China Relief Committee. There was no need to answer the letter tonight. Long ago he had stopped answering each letter when he found his days so much the same, his life changing so little. He wondered what he could say to them that would be worth while. They had worried about him more when he was on the *Hornet* than they had since he came to Guadal and there was really no difference. He hoped that Jack would go back to Andover for his last year. If he got that in, maybe the war would be over and he could go ahead to college.

Anyway the chances would be better of his going to college after the war.

Forsyth tilted back his cap and propped his elbows on the table and thought of his own years at college. He remembered walking up the hill for the first time that September evening, past the slanting row of fraternity houses, and seeing the memorial gates at the top. Beyond their old iron grillwork was University Hall, its brown bricks faded and chipped from the sun and snow of every summer and winter since before the Revolution. Walking past it, he had seen the old bronze plaque that told you Lafayette had quartered his soldiers inside and later you heard how they had torn down the woodwork and the banisters and stairs for firewood that last cold winter of the Revolution.

Back of the hall was the green plateau of the middle campus, with the ivied chapel and nursemaids with children and dogs barking and a few old men who came there in the quiet of the evening. After that the days and weeks and months were hazy and he could recall only faces and things that had happened and the way his life had changed each year as he grew up. He remembered the first Yale game and how he had driven down to New Haven in the morning and gone over to the Zete house for lunch and stood at the bar drinking Dutch beer until it was time to grab his coat and run out to the street and hop aboard one of the open trolleys. At the Bowl there had been the bands and the mascots and the guys on the team that he had seen around the campus and the parade between the halves and the kids running across the field and the famous hoax of the banner that was carried around the Bowl with the words *Cash for Old Razor Blades* and the guy's name underneath.

But later on, the games were all the same except that there was more drinking afterward, and you drove up to Northampton or Pine Manor and saw your friends in Boston or

Providence and every year there was a different girl at games and dances and a new one every week in the summer. But in the winter, when you weren't skiing at Manchester or seeing shows in New York, you hit the books until bock beer came again and you sat on the gray granite steps and drank with the others and drove out to the little Italian restaurant on Government Hill and had steamed clams and spaghetti and went down to the Yacht Club in the evenings and watched the little dinghies with white sails scudding up and down the river in the fresh breeze.

He remembered that first year, when he spoke, how his *r*'s became softened almost to *h*'s and he began consciously adding an *r* to words like *saw* and *Artie Shaw* and then he started saying them naturally and pretended he had been speaking that way all his life.

The first Christmas vacation when he had gone back to Stamford, he went to all the parties. There was a lot of good champagne and name bands and the gang that he had known at the Yacht Club and at prep school, but the girls who were on the marriage block danced with the seniors and juniors and talked about Dobbs and Ethel Walker, and that spring a lot of engagements had been announced and he went down to Block Island for the summer and worked as a life guard and drank in the evenings at Dirty Dick's. When he came back in the fall he went out for swimming and made the team as a backstroker and sometimes on Saturday afternoons a bunch of them would go over to tea dances at the girls' boarding school in town, but that year they seemed like kids and he gave it up by spring. He drove up to Northampton that March to see a girl he had met at a winter house party and they used to go to Rahar's on Saturday night and drink beer and sing *Lord Jeffrey Amherst*, and take the car over by the pond until it was time to drive back to Quad. And Sunday morning they'd open up Rahar's for ham sandwiches and brandy milk punches. By May he had given her his pin and she had asked him down to Easthampton during the summer, but somehow they had stopped writing by the end of June and his pin came in the mail one morning and he remembered taking it off the little piece of white cardboard and putting it back in his stud box.

That autumn they started giving beer parties with the Alpha Delts on Saturday afternoons—eighty of them drinking and taking turns tending bar, and a lot of laughs came from those parties—like driving up to Wellesley with five pitchers of beer in the rear of the car and finding the girls sober, and being irritated when they wanted to go to the Copley, and sitting on the running board in front of their dorm, drinking a pitcher of beer under the lamplight.

Forsyth got up and took his weapons belt from the nail and unscrewed the top of his canteen. He drank from it and put the canteen back in its canvas case, snapping it in place. He knocked the ashes from his pipe and lighted it again. The night was cool but the breeze had died down, and he sat watching the insects bumping against the bulb and the smoke from his pipe wreathing upward in the light, wishing he had a can of beer.

He thought of the night when he and the others had stayed up and driven between Williamstown and Amherst and Holyoke and parked in the Quad at Northampton at dawn and shaved beside the car with the mist still on the walls of the dorms and fell asleep after breakfast in the car in front of the Draper Hotel. That had been a good spring, he remembered, with the Prom coming late, when they could wear white dinner coats, and the cocktail parties at the houses and lobster at the Middle Street Tavern and the girl he had from Boston who wore shoulder-length white kid gloves. He had hardly seen her because all the guys wanted to meet her. She had been in love with him, but he had begun to think about law school and she had too much money to be contented living with him in Cambridge for three years while he studied.

Junior summer he had gone abroad. The boat sailed early in June, and he had gone home for three days before he went down to New York to meet the other guys. They had spent a night in Manhattan, and in the morning they took a taxi over to Hoboken and got on the *Kungsholm*. Bud Converse was in the cabin with him and when the ship sailed in the afternoon they stood on the boat deck listening to the band play *Anchors Aweigh* until they were out of the harbor and then they went in to the bar and drank for a while and watched the deck games and got their table number from the purser.

They ate at second sitting, and there was a big table of smorgasbord and when he had filled his plate he went back to the table and opened a bottle of sauterne. While he was drinking he saw her sitting three tables away. He remembered putting the glass down and watching the girl between her father and mother, and Bud Converse said, *"Someone you know?"* and he said, *"Yes, but I don't know her name."* And he had sat there watching her until she got up to leave and after a while he had gone to the ballroom looking for her, but she was not there and he had met the others in the bar with girls and they had stayed there drinking until four. In the morning, when he walked around deck, he had looked for her again and had not found her until the afternoon, when he walked past the ping-pong table. A ball had bounced down on the deck and he brought it out of the scuppers and gave it back to her, and the girl she was playing with went away and they stood there without saying anything until the steward came up to them with the tea cart and they sat next to each other in deck chairs and ate little frosted cakes and drank tea and he could remember how she looked sitting there beside him with the wind blowing the ends of the handkerchief around her dark-brown hair and then she said, *"My name's Linda Chapin. Hello,"* and he said, *"I'm Eliot Forsyth,"* and she told him she was from Memphis and after a while they got up and played ping-pong but he couldn't keep his mind on the game because he wanted to tell her that he'd been looking for her for a lifetime and now that he'd found her, couldn't they just talk?

As he sat alone in his tent near Henderson Field he thought of her laugh, as light as her first kiss that night after the dance when they sat on the boat deck in the mists of the Atlantic. All of the nights afterward they had gone there until the ship was at the North Cape, anchored in the fjord. The boats went into the landing, but she wasn't supposed to climb because she was just recovering from appendicitis, and they wrote postcards in the little windswept hut and she licked stamps for him and followed him up the trail to the top of the Cape. She tired quickly and he had to wait for her while the others went ahead. Bud Converse was with the girl from Scarsdale. When Linda had rested a little, he took off his trench coat and made her wear it and brought out the pint of whiskey he had been saving and they drank it together, their arms around each other, and it had warmed them against the biting wind. Finally they had reached the top of the plateau where the bare rock stretched out for miles and the wind seemed to come straight from the Pole as they walked toward the little shack that had been built for the tourists. The others had built a fire, and the wind was blowing gusts of smoke into the single crowded room, and the waiters from the ship poured cognac into paper cups for everybody and they stood by the fire, feeling its warmth, listening to the people laughing and talking around them, but he had not thought about the others because in all the world there was only the girl beside him, wearing a white wool sweater and a tinkling silver charm bracelet on her wrist. They had signed the register together in that little shack at the top of the world, after pushing through the milling crowd, and, finally, after more cognac, they had left and started to walk back across the top of the Cape to the trail, but he had held her arms at her side and kissed her roughly and brought her to him while the wind howled around them, and then they went slowly down the trail together, and the others caught up with them and kidded them about wanting to be alone together, but he had laughed it off the way he had grown used to.

Back aboard the ship there had been scrambled eggs and champagne for breakfast and afterward they walked around the ship in the gray morning until, sitting beside him in a deck chair, she told him that she loved him and he saw the tears in her eyes and he knew it had happened the way he had known it would all his life, and, when she left, he pulled the blanket over him and fell asleep in the chair as the ship moved quietly through the mists of the fjord.

His pipe was dead and he tapped out the ashes on his heel and laid it on the table; tomorrow evening he would have another pipeful. He had not thought about those years in a long time, but every now and then he brought out the scenes and looked at them and filed them away again in his mind. Sometimes he wanted to forget them, but tonight he wanted to remember every detail. Four years, he thought. It's been four years since that summer and I still think about it. . . .

He looked at his pipe lying before him, with the inlaid class numerals 40 on the bowl. He had got it the end of his junior year and taken it abroad with him. Linda had never liked it, so he had stopped smoking it for a while, until they got to London and he wanted to try some English tobacco. There had been Simpson's and the Savoy and cocktails at the Grosvenor House with her mother and father and then they had gone to Paris and had brandy and *croissants* on Sunday morning under the trees at the de la Paix, and then at Lorry Park in Copenhagen there had been the open-air café in the evening, with the blue and red balloons in the trees, and the fiddler who played on the stage with his band and joked with the people at the little tables and they had drunk *akvavit* and beer from glasses shaped like boots. He had brought one back as a souvenir. His money had begun to go, so that when they went back to London he had to travel third class. He remembered getting on the train at the Gare du Nord and buying bread and warm champagne at the stops on the way to Boulogne and when they got on the channel steamer she stood out on the deck with him in the rain until they docked at Folkestone, and he went to the Russell Square and they met at the Grosvenor House every day.

One night when they walked through Hyde Park, the barrage balloons were up and sirens wailed and the lights went out everywhere, and he thought of how they had stood under the trees looking up at the silver-gray barrage balloons only three days before the war, when they were very much in love.

He knew that he could never again be as happy as he had been on the crossing. The ship was dark, but that made it easier for them to be alone, and every night the band played a beautiful arrangement of "On the Alamo" and they always danced together and sat at a little table at the edge of the floor and talked about getting married in the spring.

It brought a lump to this throat now that he was thinking about it again, but, since he had started, he wanted to think it through and then try to forget it for a while.

In Quarantine, off New York, they had sat together on a hatch cover and watched the lights of the city all through that last night. The tugboats in the harbor passed by and in the full moon they had seen the man sitting on deck smoking and she had turned her lips to him and he knew that she wanted him, but he had said, "Not just for tonight, darling. I want it to be for always," and she had said nothing and later they walked around the boat deck together for the last time and kissed good night by the *salon* and he went back to the hatch and sat on it, smoking a cigarette, watching the skyline and the silhouettes of the ships going in and out of the harbor.

Forsyth remembered sitting on his baggage at Customs, feeling hot and sweaty and unshaven and seeing the guy from Memphis meet her. She had noticed him watching and came over to tell him not to be silly; he was only a boy she had grown up with, that she *had* to be nice to; she was going to marry you. And you kissed her good-bye, away from her parents, and she wrote you every day for a while, but then, when she was getting ready for her coming-out party, you couldn't get there because of a Political Science exam that meant a lot toward getting into Harvard Law.

The only picture he ever had of her had gone down on the *Hornet.* It was very sweet and restrained, but he had noticed the suggestion of hardness around her mouth.

He did not see her until next summer, in Newport, after graduation, and they had sat in his car and she had told him, and he remembered the sound of her voice as though someone had broken a champagne glass and the little pieces tinkled and chimed together, and for the first time the pain had come around his heart and he had looked away and driven her back.

Now, as he sat under the staring light, he thought of the softness of her mouth when she kissed him that last time and left before his tears had come, and he turned and looked beyond the walls of his tent into the night. I remember, darling, he thought. I'll always remember. . . .

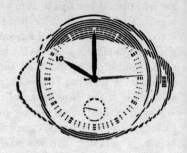

*B*ABE CAME INTO THE TENT AND SAW FORSYTH SITTING ALONE
at the table. He turned off his flashlight and walked over to
him.

"Hello," he said. "Back from the movie."

"Oh," Forsyth said, startled at hearing the other's voice.

"Did you write any letters?"

"No," Forsyth said, "I didn't get around to it."

Babe sat down on his cot. He wondered what Forsyth had
been doing while he was gone. "The picture was pretty good,"
he said.

"What made it so long?" Forsyth asked.

"The projector kept breaking down, and it took them a long
time to change reels."

"I haven't been for a long time," Forsyth said. "Maybe I'll
go tomorrow night. What's playing, *Birth of a Nation*?"

"Might be," Babe said. "They didn't announce it."

"Feel tired?"

"Not so much now. I'll write Marge a letter and turn in.
Will the light bother you?"

"No," Forsyth said. "Go ahead. Better knock off soon or you won't get your beauty sleep."

"I had a nap before dinner," Babe said. "I feel better now."

"I'll get in my sack," Forsyth said. "I haven't done a damn thing since chow." He got up from the table and went over to his cot.

"How are your folks?" Babe asked.

"Good," Eliot said. "I think they've finally stopped worrying about me."

"How's that?"

"They figure it's safer here than on the *Hornet*," Eliot said. "Maybe they're right."

"Will I ever get carrier duty?" Babe asked.

"Probably, but not for a while. We'll finish our tour of duty here and go back to the States. Some of us will get duty instructing and the skipper may go to a new carrier as air officer. They might build a squadron around Lambert."

"But he's not very old."

"No," Eliot said, "but he grew up fast. The only things he takes seriously is killing Japs and flying. Out here he can combine the two. He doesn't worry about anything else."

"I wish I could be like that," Babe said.

"It's a good way to be. The reason he's a good flier is that there isn't anything else on his mind. When he came to the Pacific he left nothing behind."

"The picture was *The Gold Rush*," Babe said abruptly.

"In sound?" He wondered why Babe had changed the subject.

"Yes . . . pretty scratchy."

Eliot took off his shoes and got under the netting. He listened for mosquitoes, and, when he decided that there were none, he tucked the netting underneath the mattress and lay back on the pillow. He closed his eyes and for a while he thought of that night in the Baltic when Linda had stood beside him at the rail, watching the three-masted schooner sailing slowly against the bright yellow moon on the rim of the sea.

Babe watched Forsyth lying under the shadow of his netting and when he heard him breathing regularly he went over to the table and sat down. He saw Forsyth's weapons belt hanging up and knew that he had forgotten to clean his .45. Babe had put the things from Kokumbona under his cot in a little pile, and he looked at them and decided not to bother with them tonight. Tomorrow he'd put them in the sun and let them dry before cleaning them. Maybe one of the mechs would make him a wooden box so that he could ship them home. There were two light grenades that Bud had unfused, a rusty Luger, a flag, a water bottle, fourteen rounds of .25 rifle ammunition and a helmet with two bullet holes. He had wanted to try out his carbine, so he had shot the helmet on the ground. The impact of the bullet kicked it ten feet into the air and rolled it down into an overgrown gulley where he had waded after it.

The letters from Marge were still in his pocket. Each had said almost the same thing. She missed him . . . when was he coming home . . . an allotment check had been four days late and she had begun to worry . . . she was lonesome without him . . . some of the other wives were going out with other men but she never would . . . it had been a mistake about the baby and anyway she would have been afraid unless he could be there when it was born. He felt a little empty as he sat there and looked at the pile of old magazines on the far corner of the table. For a while he had thought of himself as a father and it made him feel older and more confident, but now that was gone and he wondered if he wouldn't be better off if he hadn't married. The other guys seemed to get along all right—like Lambert and the skipper and Forsyth. He looked at Eliot, who had turned on his side and pulled the blanket around his shoulders. He was going to tell the story about the girl who was married to somebody else. Babe guessed he had forgotten about it. He would ask him again, the next time they had a drink at the Commander's tent.

The mosquitoes had been bad at the Cocoanut Bowl during the picture. He looked at his forearms and saw that there were several red welts. There had been some bites on his neck when he was watching the picture and he knew that there must be malaria in his bloodstream by now. He would remember to take atabrine every day.

He thought of the torpedo inside the bomb bay of his plane and wondered if he would be able to get a ship tonight. He must think to put on his dark glasses just before starting the run, so that the searchlights would not blind him the way they had the first night. The second time, when he dropped mines, the lights had not got on him at all; they had converged up-stairs on a B-17, and he had been able to lay his mines and bank away toward Maifu without being seen. Tonight it would be different.

Somewhere up the Slot a PBY was heading for the island where Barnes was waiting. He thought of him, crouched in the jungle or lying on a beach, waiting for the sound of the P-boat's engines before he signaled with his flashlight or built a bonfire. The Cat would circle low and land in the moonlight and a rubber dinghy would push out toward shore. Babe hoped that he would never have to wait like that. . . .

Destroy your aircraft and maps by fire, the instructions said. *Search your pockets and empty them. Don't reveal your unit, its strength or its location. Do not give in to threats.*

He took Marge's letters from his pocket and put them on the table. Tomorrow he would read them again. A chute opens in two seconds, he remembered. Nobody expects you to risk your life to save your plane. Open the cockpit hood, unfasten your safety belt, look at your ripcord, go over the side head first—toward the inside of a spin—keep your legs straight before pulling the ripcord. Check oscillation by pulling down on the rising side of the chute. Pull the shrouds in the direction you want to go. Release the harness before hitting the water, then inflate your life jacket. That was how you did it. But if he could, he would always try to bring the plane down because of the crew, landing her fully stalled with flaps down, disposable load jettisoned and bomb bays closed, landing gear retracted, navigational and interior lights on. Get out fast and inflate the raft, keeping it lashed to you. Put out the sea anchor. . . .

Then there were the things in the pockets of the raft: the fluorescein dye and the fishing tackle and smoke grenade and the emergency rations. Babe lighted a cigarette and was glad he had made the crew practice getting out the raft over by the revetment. He was not worrying about this strike, but it was good to check over those things now so that he could concentrate on the final briefing. He looked at his watch. He would have to turn in soon and he wondered if he could get to sleep before it was time to get dressed for the strike.

In the summertime, on his uncle's farm, there had never been things like that to think about—just getting up early, and going into the fields, and hoeing between the rows of corn, as the stalks climbed higher each day, and picking peas and beans and eating with the two hired men and getting fodder into the silo and hay into the loft, and going into town on Saturday night and walking along Main Street looking into the lighted windows, and having a soda at the drugstore and going to Normans' Theatre for the weekly Western. Afterward, walking back to the truck you saw the lights go out one by one and the butchers and grocerymen carried their trash out to the side-walk, and girls walked by with their mothers, and you stood in front of the truck with your hands in your pockets, feeling the night air at your throat where your collar was open, and you got into the truck and waved to the cop on the corner and drove back over the eight dark miles to Uncle Dan's farm.

But in the fall, when you went home again, there was always the Halloween Dance in the high-school gym and Marge went as Columbine and you wore a pirate's costume with a black moustache that tickled your upper lip, and the gym had been hung with orange-and-black streamers and at the intermission you found a seat for Marge and stood in line at the cafeteria for cider and doughnuts and went out and talked with your folks and your teachers and sat beside Marge and thought about the football game next Saturday. In the locker room, the guys kidded you about taking Marge out all the time, but even then they must have known that you'd marry her, and when they cut in it was because they liked her.

Sometimes after school you'd go up to the garage and talk with the mechanics and bring your flivver in and they'd know what was wrong and show you how to fix it and grind the valves each spring and sometimes you'd drive to the airport and watch the planes landing and taking off and wish that you had money enough to take lessons and learn how to fly and maybe buy a plane, and then suddenly it was graduation and you sat in the auditorium and Janie Young sang her solo and Thomas Linkem played the piano and, in white ducks and a blue flannel coat, you got your diploma and you were going to State for agriculture. In your second year there, Marge came, and that winter you walked with her through the snow to her sorority house and stood on the steps with the snow falling around you and on her hair as you kissed good night.

That spring your number had come up and Professor Agnew said the Navy might be worth trying and so you signed up and finished the year and went away to Primary Flight and Marge had cried because she wanted you to stay out if you could, and you went from Corpus Christi to Pensacola to Alameda, and she had come out, and in the chapel at the Air Station the chaplain had married you and you drove to San Francisco and stayed at the St. Francis. Afterward it was nice to come home to the apartment and smell the steak in the oven and kiss her in the flowered apron she always wore and you did the dishes together and went out to a movie or to a hotel when you wanted to dance, but she didn't like to drink and you always hated to pay the cover or the minimum when she only sipped two Cokes all evening.

At Pearl you stayed in B.O.Q. and went to the Moana with the others on Saturday nights, and sunned at the Royal Hawaiian on Sunday afternoons and wondered how it had been in peace time.

And from there you had gone to Fiji and made patrol flights twice a day and lined up at the bar in the big thatched clubhouse, waiting for it to open so that you could get a bottle of cold pineapple juice, and some of the natives posed beside you for a picture you sent back to Marge. Every day on the long veranda there'd be new guys who were coming back, and you tried to talk to them at first, but they just wanted to sit there looking out over the hills until it was time for chow again, and finally you moved on to Tontouta and once a week you got in to Noumea and went to the Pacifique and drank beer and watched the ships in the harbor and walked up and down the dusty streets looking at the little Javanese women with cone-shaped straw hats and babies on their backs, and every day you felt a little closer to the war.

One day when you had just landed, a P-38 overshot the field

and plowed into the stumps at the end and a piece of metal from the explosion had nicked your wing, but in a couple of days they had dragged the wreck away and you never saw what they did with the pilot's body. Mail was hard to get with your P. O. number changing every month or so, and once in a while you'd get a stack of old letters that had gone to Pearl or Nandi, but they were good to read too and it made you anxious to go up north to Guadal so that you could get the job finished and get back to Marge.

Babe heard Forsyth start in his sleep and saw him roll over until his hand hit the netting, but his eyes did not open and he began to breathe evenly again. I wonder what he was dreaming about, Babe said to himself. I always thought he slept like a log.

He listened to the night and it struck him that he had never heard a bird sing since leaving Hawaii. He had seen a lot of birds on the islands, and in the jungle today there had been white cockatoos screaming harshly as he broke through the vines on the jungle floor. Bud had shot at one, but the bullet was low and the bird flew away between the high branches above. Then they had stumbled on a field-piece that the Japs had dragged up into the hills. It had an English name-plate, but the markings had been stamped over with Japanese characters and Bud said they must have taken it from Singapore. It was painted brown and green and yellow and you had hardly seen it at the side of the trail but there were no shells with it and they had left it and walked on.

Babe got up from the table, feeling the cramped muscles of his thighs, and took a sheet of paper from his stationery box. He went back to the table and began writing a letter to his wife. He told her that he missed her and that he loved her and he hoped she could find things or friends to fill her time until he was home again. When he made j.g. he would make out a larger allotment to her and not to worry if it didn't come through right away.

He didn't say anything about the baby, but he thought for a moment that he might say something about having one when he came back. He looked at the unfinished letter and decided just to add that he was beginning to get used to it out here and that if he wasn't back by fall, he'd like her to go back to State until he could get leave. He could not think of anything else to say, so he signed the letter and folded it and put an air-mail stamp on the envelope and put it on the table in front of him. He'd drop it in the mail box on the way to chow at noon.

A rat ran across the floor near the edge of the tent and he wondered whether they ought to have a rat trap. He knew that Cordell had made one out of a bucket helmet, and some fighter pilots rigged one from an electric grid hooked to an old jeep battery. They had told him it worked fine but that you had to get the dead rat off the grid right away or he started to roast and smelled up the tent.

He reached up and began to unscrew the light bulb. It was hot and he turned it a little at intervals so that he would not burn his hand, and then he twisted it once more and the light went out and he could see the moon shining in through the door of the tent.

Sitting on the side of his cot, he took off his shoes and socks and raised the netting and lay back on top of the blanket, thinking of the days that had gone by, when he drove in from the farm on Saturday night and watched the people walking in front of the stores under the light of the street lamp, standing in the shadows with his collar open and the cool night wind at his throat.

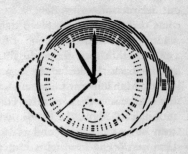

*H*ERE'S MINE, BEN," ONE OF THE SBD PILOTS SAID.

"Thanks, Jake," Lambert said. He stuck the twenty-dollar bill in his pocket with the rest of his winnings.

They were standing around a pair of tables that had been pushed together in the center of the tent floor. Poker chips were scattered on the top of the table and one of the younger pilots gathered them up.

"How much'd you take, Ben?" somebody asked.

"Something over two hundred," he said.

The pilot groaned. "And I'm due for Auckland in three weeks."

"It's your turn next," Ben said. He took the cap from his belt and put it on his head.

"We hate to let you go," Jake said.

Ben laughed. "The war won't wait," he said. "I'm flying tonight."

"Don't drop that lettuce over Kahili," Jake said. "Anything else goes."

"Right," Ben said. "Let me know the next time you need easy money."

"See you tomorrow, Ben."

"Good night, gents. Sleep tight." He pushed aside a seat and walked toward the door of the tent.

Outside, he took the flashlight from his belt, and, shining it on the grass, walked to the jeep. He got in and turned on the headlights. The seat was damp with condensed moisture, and the engine started sluggishly. He could hear them inside the tent, talking about the hands they had held. Ben turned the jeep out to the road and started slowly back toward the squadron. The headlights knifed out cleanly ahead of the jeep, cutting through the mists that were beginning to rise from the darkness at the side of the road. As he rounded a bend, the lights flashed through a grove of palms and he thought that their evenly spaced gray trunks looked like a field of telephone poles.

Playing table stakes, the ensigns had lost as usual. Most of them had never played poker until they joined the Navy, and now that they were where money meant nothing, they tried to win more. Hell, if they wanted to play tomorrow, he'd give them a game. The windshield lay forward over the hood, and the morning air rustled his shirtsleeves and flapped the points of his collar. It was much cooler than when he had driven over earlier in the evening. He had forgotten to bring a flight jacket to wear back. It would be a hell of a note if he got a malaria chill because of a poker game he hadn't wanted to play, but Jake and he had been ensigns on the *Enterprise* until just before Midway and they had played poker together in the wardroom and drunk coffee between flights—just about a year ago, he thought. He remembered sitting in the ready room that afternoon waiting to go and then the words had come over the loudspeaker *Launch the Attack Group*, and the planes had come up on the elevators from the hangar deck and the deck crews had wheeled them into position, and he had climbed up on the wing of his plane and looked back at the sea of whirling props. Inside the cockpit, he had sat gripping the stick and waggling the rudder nervously until they flagged him away and he gunned the plane and rolled down the deck past the island and the men clasping their hands over their heads and then he was off the deck and the carrier was behind and he had banked and climbed to join the others.

The jeep bumped over a bad section of the road and he remembered the sea of mud that had been there two months ago. He slowed the jeep and raised his head, letting the wind blow inside his shirt.

Then they had gone down on their run and he had seen Jerry and Mort and Sam knocked down and he had jockeyed lower and got ready and then Flash and Bert blew up beside him and he saw the stuff breaking around him and he steadied her, feeling the wind from the open bays whistling around his legs, and then his right thumb pressed the little red button on top of the stick and the fish was away and he turned to climb and the left wing splintered and he heard the gunner cry out and he had jammed the stick to the right, fighting to keep her up level, but she had dropped and he brought up the nose as much as he could and the tail struck first and then the water was swirling over the hood and he pushed it back drunkenly and pulled the inflating cords on his jacket and fought out of the cockpit against the water around his body, and the plane sank and he had looked for Hart and Nielson, but they hadn't got out, and he realized his head must have hit the panel because there was blood in the water around him and the warm salt water stung his forehead. Ahead of him the big carrier had burned and lost speed as she began her death circle. The men on her decks looked like frantic rats as they climbed over her, trying to stay away from the sea, but she had listed and the stern came up slowly at first and then the bow went down and the steam rushed out of her stacks and she was gone quickly under the froth of the sea. And there had been the whine of planes above him and when he looked up a Zero was coming in to strafe and he had ducked under the surface and heard the first burst tear into the water beside him and when it was gone he looked again and saw it roll over for another try and he went under again as it came screaming down from the sun and then his arm went limp and his back and his thigh burned where the burst had hit him and he saw little tendrils of blood float up around his body, and the pain in his leg had come and he wondered if the bone was broken, and held his thigh, trying to stop the bleeding because of the sharks, and where the carrier had gone down a monstrous bubble had surged up, breaking the surface and he wondered if it was Sam's or Mort's or his torpedo that did it, and then he looked up in the sky at the planes careening high above the smoke of the ships and the white and black bursts of the ack-ack, and the sea was warm against his body and he felt tired and his eyes were heavy and the waves picked him up and rolled him and dropped him easily between the crests as though he were going down a slide into a sand pile the way he had when he was a kid, only there was nothing under his feet, and his arms had felt weak and his head lolled back in the water as he closed his eyes against the glare of the afternoon sun. . . .

Lambert shook his head sharply, and brought the jeep over to the center of the road. The Squadron sign whitened in the headlights as he turned into the road between the palms. The tents were dark and he drove slowly so that the sound of the engine would not wake any of the others. He wished he had been able to leave the game earlier; now there would be hardly time to turn in. He dimmed the lights as he drove up to his tent and turned off the ignition, coasting the rest of the way. He turned off the lights and sat looking at the moon over the tops of the palms. It had been full last night, but tonight it was still almost perfect, and he knew that it would be bright over Kahili. He could see the steps in the moonlight and he opened the door quietly and went into the tent.

Standing beside the table, he struck a match and lighted the candle. It glowed into life, shadowing him against the side of the tent, and he saw that Cordell was already asleep. Ben sat down on the chair as the candle flared higher, and saw Joe's letter beside his Reising gun on the table. He took his weapons belt from the cot and pulled his .45 from its holster. He pressed the little button and the magazine slid out into his hand. He saw that it was full, and pressed it back. He pulled the breech until he heard a shell click into the chamber. Then he eased it forward until it stopped and clicked on the safety. He returned the pistol to its holster, and, closing the flap, put the belt on the table before him. He looked at his watch; they would be calling him in fifteen minutes.

He looked around the darkened tent at the things that were his. Not a hell of a lot to show for twenty-three years, he thought—an empty Burgundy bottle, a sea chest full of old khakis and skivvies. Some old letters wrapped with a piece of cord, an ash tray from the *Lex*, the billfold in his pocket, the silver identification chain on his right wrist, his wrist watch and class ring—not much for twenty-three years of living.

The first time they had let him out of sick bay he had gone up to the wardroom for dinner. The others were quiet when he sat down alone at the table that had been his squadron's. It was hard to eat that night, sitting by yourself, looking at the long table with the white cloth over it and the empty chairs around it, seeing the other tables in the wardroom with only a few missing here and there.

He remembered flying east from the Mare Island Hospital for ten days' sick leave. The first few days, when he stayed with his mother and father, he slept most of the time and kept away from people who came to see him and ask him what it was like. Then he had taken the train to Boston and gone down to the Cape to stay at their old place. It was the end of summer then and most of the people had gone back to Sewickley and Shaker Heights and Brookline and New York, so when he went down to the beach that first morning it was the way he had always remembered it—the wide stretch of white sand between the two jutting points of rock and a few beach umbrellas back in the dunes—and he had walked down from the beach club and stretched out on the sand and let the sun reach his scars. After a while he had gone in and swum out to the point and rested on a rock with the spray blowing over him. From there you could see the people coming down to the beach with their chairs and towels and beach mats and big straw hats and he had watched them until it was time to go back and have lunch with his brother.

He remembered walking along the asphalt road and feeling its heat under the soles of his sneakers, past the Northland Hotel with its unpainted shutters and old brown shingles, until he turned up the drive to the house where he had lived almost every summer of his life.

Jeff had sat with him on the porch, looking out over the rocks, watching the people he did not know walk past, but it was hard to talk to Jeff because he still lived in the world you had moved away from and begun to forget. So after a while, you went down to the beach alone and walked behind the dunes, through the wild sea grass that waved in the offshore breeze, and the sun felt good on your back and arms and you found a place to lie down, away from the others, and fell asleep in the sun until some kids playing ball near by woke you. You sat up, looking out over the ocean, hardly believing that you were back again on the beach of your childhood—away from the planes and the sinking ships and the screams of the dying men—and the little Star boat offshore came about and headed into the wind close-hauled, but it was not one you knew, and you took off your sneakers and walked down to the water, feeling the warm sand between your toes, and you ran head first into the waves and swam until you were tired. Then you had come out of the water and stood at the edge of the beach, brushing the water off your body and shaking the water from your hair.

As you walked up to the sand, you saw her lying on a blanket with her mother and father and there was a baby beside her, but before you had made up your mind, Mr. Anderson had seen you and stood up and waved to you to come over and you had felt the tightness in your stomach again, the way you always did when you saw her. She had seen you before you reached them and sat up, holding her suit top because the straps were down and she had smiled at you and said, *Hello, Ben. It's been so long since I've seen you.* And her father had shaken hands with you and her mother had taken off her dark glasses and said how much thinner you were and the baby on the blanket crawled toward the sand and Jean had reached out and brought it back and her skin had never been so tanned before, but the baby looked white and had blonde hair, and they said they'd missed you last summer and you said that you'd missed being back and her mother said, my, but a lot of things must have happened to you, Ben, as she lay back and put on some more tanning lotion, and Jean asked you how long you'd been back and you said just since last evening and she told you that they had been staying at the hotel this summer and their house was closed because there were no servants to be had anywhere. Mr. Anderson said it seemed funny this summer not to see you and Jean going over to the hotel together for the dances the way you always had, and you looked at her baby and began to hate it because it was not part of you the way it should have been, and Jean said it was too bad you hadn't come back sooner because they were leaving the hotel at five to go back home, and the baby began to cry and Mrs. Anderson sat up and said she thought she'd had enough sun for the summer and anyway the baby ought to have its nap, and she gathered up her things and lifted the baby and walked down the beach and Mr. Anderson looked at you and asked you to drop around and have a drink for old times' sake, but you said you thought Jeff had something lined up, thanks anyway, and he shook your hand again and said how good it was to see you and you could see him looking at your scars and then he walked away after his wife. ·

Ben remembered sitting there beside the girl he had loved all the summers of his life, while she slid the straps over her shoulders and put the top back on the bottle of lotion. Then she had asked what the matter was and there was nothing to say, so she asked you about the *Lex* going down and there was nothing you wanted to say, and you looked at her lovely face and the golden-brown hair falling down over her shoulders and finally you asked her if she was happy and she said she was worried that Roger might be drafted and she had been thinking about writing you and asking you to help him get a commission—his eyes weren't very strong— so maybe he could get into the Supply Corps or whatever it was. But she didn't look at you when she spoke, and the bitterness that had been in your heart so long burst out and you told her that you didn't give a goddamn what happened to Roger and if he'd gone in when you had, he wouldn't have been hanging around to marry her the first summer you were away. You could see that she was frightened because she had said the wrong thing and you wanted to hate her, the way you hated her baby, but now that you were with her nothing remained of the hate you had tried to create while you were away.

You saw the little sailboat turning out toward sea and thought of the afternoons when her father had sat in his bed-room getting drunk with you and saying he'd be damned glad to see you in the family, and you felt her hand on your arm and when you looked in her eyes it was the same way she had looked when you danced together in the hotel and at the Canoe Club, but you knew that her life was patterned now and she had been trapped, and she talked to you unsteadily and said it had been her mother who had never liked you because you were too much like her father, and you got to your feet and looked at her and said *Good-bye, sweetheart,* very softly and turned to go down the beach and she was crying a little as you walked away past the beach umbrellas and the people you did not know, past the big frame hotel, down the walk past the rocks, and into the yard where Jeff was sitting on the front porch drinking beer with his wife. . . .

Ben heard somebody knock at the door. He got up from the table and opened it. It was the orderly from Strike Command.

"It's time, Mr. Lambert," he said.

"Thank you," Ben said. "I'll wake Mr. Cordell."

The candle had burned low, and the melting wax ran down the sides of the old Burgundy bottle, making little white pools on the table. As he took down his flight suit from the nail, he knew that he could never forget the way that summer had ended.

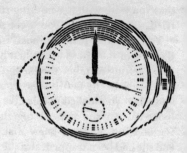

DRIVING OVER THE ROUGH ROAD, CORDELL AND LAMBERT SAW
the lights of the jeeps in the valley ahead of them. There was
a cluster of lights around the weather shack on top of Pagoda
Hill where the jeeps were parked and they drove up the side
of the hill and stopped. The weather shack was made from
two Dallas huts joined together, and had screened windows.

They saw the others inside, getting out their Nav boards
and talking with the weather sergeant, and Lambert opened
the door for Cordell and followed him into the room. Most
of the others were there already, dressed for the strike. They
wore loose tan flight suits that were pulled together at the
waist by heavy weapons belts, white silk scarves, gabardine
helmets with built-in sponge-rubber earphones, and gloves in
the bulging map pockets below their knees. Some of them
carried yellow life jackets over their shoulders, and a few were
getting into them. Lambert had sprayed his blue so that he
would be harder to strafe. A few of them wore shoulder
holsters, made of tooled leather or canvas sewn together at the
parachute loft. Their weapons belts carried one or two canteens, a .45 and two extra clips, a first-aid case, a flashlight in a

canvas case fastened to the belt by a lanyard, and a sheath knife. Already some of them had put their night binoculars around their necks where they hung from a shortened leather strap. There were benches around the room, and at one end a large drafting table where the weather charts were drawn.

The officers seated themselves and lighted cigarettes and talked until the weather sergeant stepped to the center of the floor.

"Gentlemen," he said, "if you'll give me your attention, I have a few things of interest to you."

They stopped talking and took notepaper from their map pockets and prepared to write against the hard transparent surface of the Nav boards across their knees.

"Your altitude will be 8,000 feet until just before the attack, so this dope holds good for that altitude. Excellent visibility with scattered clouds below you at 4,500 feet. The wind will be from zero-eight-oh at eighteen knots. This'll give you a break on the way up. Coming back at 5,000 feet there'll be moderate visibility with light cloud formations as far as Russell."

"How about the Army?" one of the pilots asked. "Do they have the word?"

"Yes, sir. They've been briefed. They ought to be taking off any minute."

As he spoke, they heard the grinding roar of a bomber's engines as the first one started down the runway.

"I hope they find it tonight," somebody said.

The sergeant continued. "You know the homing dope. The Hudson will be dropping flares from 5,000 feet every five minutes, and your radiomen can call the field on the regular liaison channel if you're lost or in trouble. Maintain radio silence as usual at least until inside the hundred-mile arc. If you don't know where Henderson is or your gas is low, give us a call on Liaison and we'll send out a guide plane for you or you can try to land at Russell. That's all, gentlemen. Good luck."

McRae nodded at the sergeant and took the center of the floor. "It looks like a good night," he said calmly. "Course will be two-nine-three and speed as usual. The tail wind will give us a break on gas, but don't figure it too closely. If something happens so that we can't go in the mine-carrying planes we'll return at once. Planes with torpedoes will go to Rekata Bay in case they've got some barges offshore. The five planes with bombs will dump them on the runway at Vila. Here are target maps for each of you, so pass them around and get familiar with them. See you all at breakfast."

The field telephone rang and the sergeant answered it. He turned to McRae. "Condition Red, sir." He rang off and turned off the light over his drawing table. "Lights out, gentlemen," he said. "Let's hope Charlie doesn't stay too long."

Lambert turned to Babe. "Charlie wants to break up the strike," he said. "It's lucky we weren't taking off."

Cordell went outside to turn off the jeep lights, and the lights in the room went out.

"We'd better get near a foxhole, Babe." Lambert got up and walked toward the door behind the crowd of officers who were going outside. He could hear the last bomber as it took off and climbed over the dark jungle, heading for Kahili.

They followed the others outside and saw that the searchlights were already picketing the western end of Henderson. The crews were standing in their lorries watching the sky and some of the officers sat comfortably in jeeps looking at the moving lights.

There was a slit trench on the other side of the road. A lorry was parked near it and Lambert could hear the men talking as he and Babe walked past it: ". . . so this boot, right out of camp, gets a battlewagon, and he's standin' on the fantail by himself when the Old Man walks by and sees him crapped out. The skipper walks over to him and the boot waves his hand, friendly like, and says, 'Hi, Bud. Nice boat, ain't it?' and the Old Man sputters and says, 'You must be drunk,' and the boot says *Drunk?* Hell. I been all over the whole damn boat an' there ain't a drink on it.'" The men laughed, and Lambert smiled a little at the familiar story.

Cordell came over to them. They could see him easily in the clear moonlight and the muzzle of his Reising gun glinted palely as it swung from his shoulder. The starting noise of a TBF engine echoed up to them from the revetment area.

"It's got a cough," Cordell said. "Must be mine." He sat on the ground and let his legs dangle into the slit trench. "This is a hell of a note. I'd like to get going."

"So would I," Lambert said. "I'm getting tired of waiting."

They could hear the thin muffled drone of an engine high above them.

"What's that?" Babe asked. "Are they here already?"

"No," Lambert said. "That's a night fighter."

"Do they do much good?"

"Sometimes," Lambert said. "That reminds me. Charlie may have some night fighters over Kahili tonight, so when you start back—keep your gunner on the lookout. Their black paint makes them hard as hell to see. Don't let any of them follow you back."

"I'll remember," Babe said. The phones hurt his ears and he pushed his helmet back on the top of his head, the way the others had. Some of them were smoking, cupping the glow of the cigarettes in their hands. Another TBF started in the distance and they could hear two or three crewmen clap and cheer.

"Watch the lights," Cordell said.

Lambert saw that the searchlights were converging. Some of the beams tilted slowly and others fell quickly across the sky like poles that had been severed at their base. The rays fixed themselves in a huge flexible triangle whose apex moved searchingly across the sky. Then they heard the first burst of ack-ack and the other guns began firing and there were streams of tracers pouring up from the darkness, and shells that burst like rockets above the lights and they could see the first bomber in the lights, flying slowly like a blinded insect, and two more came above it in a Vee, and there was a burst that seemed to be in the middle of them, but the planes came on and suddenly the firing had stopped and they could hear the hum of the planes coming toward them out of the night. But above them there was a high-pitched whine that knifed down out of the sky and a brief burst of tracers stabbed in the side of the first bogie. Flames seared through it, and then there was another fleck of orange light as the second burst hit it and the plane blew up in the searchlights and part of the wing came down and the plane spun out of the triangle of light, its flames wrapping it in a brilliant shroud until it hit the jungle, stunning them with its detonation, and flames showered high above the dark outline of the trees.

The lights had lost the two other bombers and a string of bombs burst somewhere in the distance. The triangle changed into separately seeking fingers that found a cloud here and there in the sky, but the bombers had turned and gone and for a moment the lights waved wildly through the sky and died away and then there was only the sky and the moonlight silhouetting the little weather shack on Pagoda Hill.

A light went on inside the shack and Lambert could hear McRae's voice.

"Condition Green. Let's go." The lights of his jeep went

on and his engine started and the jeep pulled away and rumbled down the hill toward the road that led to the revetments.

"Okay, Ben," Cordell said. "Let's get going." He shifted his Reising gun to his other shoulder as he walked to the jeep and got in.

Ben held their Nav boards across his thighs as they waited for the tangle of little cars to clear itself. One of the lorries groaned into gear and the men cheered. A plane roared into life down by the field and Ben waved at Forsyth and Babe in the other jeep as they pulled ahead of them and bounced down the narrow road.

Lambert could see lights going on again in the bivouac areas. The briefing room atop Strike Command glowed brightly before the side of Pagoda Hill cut it from view. Ahead of them in a perfect double chain, the jeep lights darted along. The first one turned off the road and the others followed, each going to a different plane, and then their jeep was down the side of the hill, going over the road to the planes, and Lambert felt the long overhanging grasses brush his cheek when Cordell steered a little to the right.

A lorry had stopped and the men were getting out. They flicked away their cigarettes and climbed down to the road and walked along in twos or threes as the jeep passed them. Lambert could see his plane ahead in the moonlight, its engine idling and the prop turning over slowly. Cordell drove under the right wing and stopped by the side of the plane. Lambert got out and put Cordell's Nav board on the empty seat. The wash from the prop tugged at the loose ends of his scarf, and he pulled up the zipper at his neck until it rested against the bunch of silk at his throat.

"Thanks, Joe," he said. "Lay them where they'll do the most good."

"Take care of yourself," Joe said. He nodded at Ben and

they waved to each other as he pulled away and drove across the mat to his own plane.

The plane captain ducked under the wing, his flashlight shining on the taxi mat. " 'Evening, Mr. Lambert," he said.

"Hello, Chief," Ben said. "How does she look?"

"Perfect, sir. Ready to go."

Ben saw the turret gunner swinging the guns in the slipstream.

"Might as well taxi out," he said. "We're late now."

"Did Charlie do any damage?"

"We didn't hear," Ben said. "We shoved off right after the searchlights went out." He held the Nav board against his chest with one arm and put on his unlined leather gloves.

"Radioman's already inside," the Chief said. "I guess he's talking with the Tower now."

"Good," Ben said. He laid the board on the trailing edge of the wing.

"Did you get an extra ration, sir?"

"No," Ben said. "I forgot to draw it at Pagoda."

"I thought you might, sir. I got one for you." He brought out a brown waxed-paper K-Ration box.

"Thanks, Chief," Ben said. "I'll need it before morning." He put his foot on the step and his hand in the hand hole above and pulled himself up on the wing, looking aft away from the backwash. He bent down and picked up his Nav board and put it inside the cockpit in the little rack underneath the panel. Then he got into the cockpit and wedged his way into the seat, pulling aside the chute straps that were in the way.

The Chief appeared beside the hood, holding on inside the cockpit. Lambert plugged in his phones and tested the intercom with the gunner and the radioman. He waggled the stick and saw the ailerons respond. Then he pushed it forward and brought it back and the elevator surfaces dropped and raised.

When he had turned on the landing lights, he pushed the pedals with his feet and moved the throttle ahead. The engine revved up instantly and he released the brakes. He gave the plane a little right rudder and it began to move out to the taxi strip. The Chief, looking ahead, motioned him to the left and he brought the plane over. Then the Chief's hand pointed straight ahead and he gave it more throttle as she moved down past the other planes that were idling in their revetments.

He could see four planes ahead of him, going down the taxi mat, and he eased the throttle until there was a greater interval between him and the next plane. The landing lights of the planes on each side of the mat were blinding and he looked down at his instrument panel. His binoculars dangled heavily against his chest, and the top of the canteen was beginning to bore into his right hip. He moved to the left and pushed the canteen down with his right hand. It felt better and he pulled the phone from the panel and switched to Liaison: *"Tower from Flint,"* he called. *"Tower from Flint."* He pushed the throttle forward, to close up with the plane ahead. *"Flint from Tower,"* his earphones said. *"Flint from Tower, we are receiving you well. Modulation good. Acknowledge."*

Ben pressed the speaking button. *"Roger,"* he said, *"Roger."*
The plane ahead turned off the alley onto the taxi mat that ran parallel with the runway. Ben eased the throttle and patted the Chief's arm. The Chief touched his helmet in salute and Ben waved at him as he walked back on the wing and jumped to the ground. Ben looked down to see that he was clear of the tail assembly and then he pushed the throttle ahead again and turned to the left and the big plane rumbled up on the taxi strip and he felt the tail wheel bouncing the plane a little.

As he slowed, toward the end of the apron, before taxiing to the runway, he saw the first three Avengers race down the strip. There was about fifty yards between them, and they were airborne within a few seconds of each other. The plane ahead moved forward and Ben followed it to the end of Henderson. Two more TBFs streaked down the runway, their blue-gray sides gleaming in the glare of the flare-pots and the landing lights of the planes that were still waiting to go. His plane moved slowly, following the other, and then he braked it while the other roared into full throttle and shook under the terrific power of its engine. Ben pulled the hood shut and looked around at the planes behind that were leaving their revetments and trundling down the mat.

The plane ahead rolled down the runway in a swirl of dust, gathering speed, and Ben looked down the dark aisle between the flickering beads of light and pushed the throttle all the way forward.

"Flint from Tower. Flint from Tower. Go ahead. Go ahead."

Ben picked up the phone. *"Wilco,"* he said evenly. *"Wilco."*

Then, with his controls neutral, he released the brakes and felt the first slow bumping as the wheels rolled over the uneven surface of the mat. The plane accelerated quickly and the flare-pots on either side of the dark aisle blurred into a dim chain, and he brought the tail up a little and then, as he felt the wings begin to take the weight, he pulled the stick lightly and the wheels left the ground.

He held the stick back with his left hand and, picking up the phone, spoke to the tower.

"Airborne," he said. *"Airborne."*

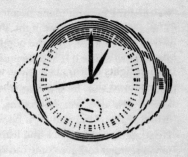

AT 400 FEET LAMBERT PULLED ON HIS CHUTE STRAPS AND fastened the safety belt. The plane was climbing steadily, and he could see the others ahead of him in the moonlight. He pulled down his goggles and slid back the hood. The cool air rushed into the cockpit, tearing at his thin helmet, beating against his wrists where the gloves were rolled down. He looked over the side and saw the dark end of Cape Esperance change into the gray of the water below. Waves broke whitely on the thin line of the beach, and he looked ahead toward Savo.

Beneath him the hulks of the *Quincy,* the *Vincennes,* the *Astoria* and the *Canberra* rotted on the floor of Iron Bottom Bay, but when he looked down—the way he always did—the surface of the water looked at rest. The long broken dorsal of Savo seemed to be even with his wingtip and as he flew past he could see the mists begin to rise, like a slow poisonous vapor, from its dark valleys.

The instrument dials glowed greenly in the dark of the cockpit and the turn-and-bank indicator showed his left wing was down a little. He brought over the stick automatically and watched the radium plane become level with the horizon line. The green landing-gear light showed that the wheels were retracted—another, that the bomb bay was closed. The planes ahead bore to the left and he pushed the pedal a little and followed them. He looked up at the compass and when they straightened out, he saw that they were paralleling the course again. His ears were becoming accustomed to the vibrant drone of the plane and soon he would not hear it any longer. He straightened his back and leaned against the headrest. The moon seemed to have come out of the ocean ahead and it was much larger than it had looked from the ground—a clear yellow-white as it rose through the thinning atmosphere. His earphones crackled and he heard McRae talking to them.

"Knucklehead to Strike. Knucklehead to Strike. Form up, stragglers."

He looked ahead and saw McRae's plane two miles beyond him at the point of the hollow spearhead that was formed by the echelon of Vees. Back of him the last few planes closed to the proper interval. Several voices were talking between planes, kidding each other, using names like Dilbert and Buster and Chico, but they were not loud enough to bother him and he knew that they would quiet down in a little while. The altimeter indicated 4,500 feet, and he could feel the wind getting cooler as they climbed. The plane at four o'clock dropped a little in an air pocket and then its nose went up and Ben could see the blue-green spurts of flame from under the cowl.

"Russell at eleven-thirty," he heard McRae say over the radio and saw its low gray outline through the sheen of his propeller arc. The first clouds were beyond Russell, but he knew that the planes would be above them when they got there. At this altitude he could not see the stars, but when he was higher the sky would seem crowded with them. His legs

were beginning to feel cramped and he moved around in his seat until the circulation started. After sitting there for four hours, the coccyx got numb and it was hard to move your legs quickly. The belt began to cut into his hips a little and he moved it around with his left hand until the knife sheath jammed against the side of the seat and stopped it.

Ben closed the hood and pushed up his goggles, blinking his eyes because of the pressure the sponge-rubber cups had made on his cheek bones. It was comfortable inside the cockpit with the hood shut, and the silk scarf felt soft around his throat. He could feel his beard scratch against the chamois lining of the chin strap. The plane dropped suddenly in an air pocket, but rose again before he needed to bring back the stick. The binoculars had bumped against his chest and he held them to his eyes and scanned the sky ahead. With the night glasses he could see the fuselage numbers of the plane to the left, where McIntyre was silhouetted against the transparent paneling of the cockpit.

Russell was much bigger below them, as they flew over the landing strip that had been hacked out of the jungle. In a few weeks, strikes would be leaving from there, and it would mean a bigger bomb load or more gas. The arrow of the altimeter pointed to 6,500 feet. He liked the long easy climb that lasted almost a hundred miles. The tip of Russell disappeared under his left wing and he looked to the right where Santa Isabel lay forty miles away, like a long crocodile with jaws that formed Rekata Bay. Charlie might have some snoopers up tonight from Rekata, but he doubted if they would jump the strike. The float planes would radio ahead to Kahili and they'd be ready for them. Hell, if the snoopers were around, they'd have seen the B-17s go by, half an hour ago. Anyway, Charlie would be wide awake when they got there.

Gatukai lay far ahead, the first of the New Georgia Islands.

Ben felt thirsty and reached around for his canteen. He un-snapped the case and pulled out the aluminum bottle and tilted it to his lips. He drank only a little, saving the rest for the trip home, when his mouth would be dry and he'd need a drink—even chlorinated water. He put away the canteen and held the stick with his other hand. It felt solid and the formed handgrip was like a Tommy-gun. That was the way to aim the plane—just pull the pistol grip a little and you could point the projectile anywhere. He thought of the 2,000-pound bomb snuggled up inside the belly of the plane a little below his feet. It was a pleasure to give it a ride, he thought. No trouble at all.

The planes ahead of him looked like little models hung from the sky by invisible wires. Now and then the moon was reflected from their hoods as the planes moved in the changing currents of air. Seventy-two hundred feet the altimeter said. Ben knew it was cold outside the panel. Eight hundred feet more and they should be almost off Vangunu. The propellers spinning in the cold clear air looked like celluloid discs pinned to the noses of the little planes. The moonlight gave them a silver sheen that made them look unreal.

The purr of the engine seemed to drop away; it was doing nicely on the lean mixture. He picked up the phone and switched to inter-com. "Pilot to gunner," he said, "keep a lookout for snoopers. We're getting near Vila."

"Aye, aye, sir," the gunner said. "I'd like permission to warm up the guns."

Lambert looked around the sky, through the rounded glass dome above his head, and through the panels on each side, and switched to Liaison. *"Strike from Flint. Strike from Flint. Testing guns. Testing guns."* He switched back to inter-com. "Fire to port," he said, "down toward the water."

The plane shook a little as the gunner swung the turret and

sprayed out a few short bursts. Lambert could hear the light pop-pop-pop of the fifties through the rush of the slipstream and then it stopped and the gunner spoke over the phones.

"Okay, sir," he said. "Turret's all set. Radioman wants to try the tail gun."

"Go ahead," Lambert said. He put the phone back in its clip on the panel. He could not hear the shooting, but the plane vibrated slightly as the recoil hammered at the tail mount. That was the only fun the boys got. He always had the crew strafe during a run because it gave them a feeling of doing something on the strike that killed Japs, and they took care of the guns better because of it. Some time he'd be jumped by a night-fighter and they'd all have their hands full. It could dive as fast as you, but it didn't dare go as close to the water. That was the thing to do—get down close to the water so that he couldn't make the kind of passes at you he wanted. If he came at you from above, where you couldn't see him, he'd never be able to pull out of the dive before he smacked into the water. If he came at you from your own altitude—hell, what were the gunners for?

He recognized Forsyth's voice singing over the phones.

"No pretty little girls to dee-cee-eve me-ee
Happy is the day when the airman gets his pay . . ."

"Pipe down, skylark," McRae's voice cut in. Lambert grinned.

"Sorry, sir. Thought I was switched off."

"Knucklehead to Snowshoe. How you making out, Joe?"

"Snowshoe to Knucklehead. Just fair, Larry."

"Strike from Knucklehead. Kolombangara in sight. Take a good look at Vila. See if you can spot any planes."

Lambert's phones went dead again, and he looked ahead at eleven o'clock and saw the broken cone of Kolombangara's crater in the distance, looming up against the gray water of the Slot. The altimeter pointed to 8,000 feet and Ben leveled off and saw that his position in formation was staying the same. *On the road to Gizo Bay,* he thought. *Where the Kawanishis play. And the flak comes up from under, out of Munda, 'cross the bay.* He wondered if anybody would collect an anthology of the doggerel that had been written at Guadal. You wrote a verse or a parody on a piece of torn paper, on the back of an ammo box, and read it to the guys in your tent and went out on a strike and got killed and the others remembered it and told it or sang it when they were drunk in Sydney or Noumea or Auckland and then everybody got to know it. Even the Red Cross girls spouted it because they thought it was terribly virile, without ever understanding why or how it had been written.

He saw Visuvisu Point below, to the left, and knew that they would be over Kula Gulf in a moment. The moon was higher, and it glinted along the cowling in front of him. The interior lights were off and the moonlight threw the shadow of the cowl padding against his life jacket. If he had needed to, he could have read his maps or figured on his Nav board without turning on the lights.

The airstrip at Vila looked chalky against the dark background of the dead volcano that was Kolombangara. He brought up his glasses and looked through the side of the hood. He could see the labyrinth of little revetments away from the strip. The base seemed dead. There were no lights and no planes on the runway. If there were any under the palms, they were too well camouflaged to be visible at night from this altitude.

While he looked, it seemed as though someone were striking matches in the distance. Tiny flames flared up beside the airstrip and disappeared into the black background, but the ack-ack was too far away to bother them. The lights appeared and disappeared at regular intervals as though a man cupped and uncupped his hand around a match below in the dark. The shells burst harmlessly away from the first Vee of planes and the formation did not change. He put both hands on the stick in case a near-by burst should bump the plane. The explosions on the ground sputtered up at them, and the shells burst a long distance from the planes. It always reminded him of Fourth of July at the park, when the fireworks burst high in the sky and the golden sparks dripped slowly toward the ground, but now he was above the bursts, watching them detonate under his left wing in grumpy red-white explosions that were farther away each time. There were no tracers, because the planes were so high, and then his plane rocked suddenly as a high burst pushed it over. Lambert brought it back to the course. That was fairly close. He picked up the phone and switched to inter-com. "Anybody hurt?" he asked.

"No, sir," the gunner said. "Charlie'll have to do better than that."

The firing was slowing down. There was only an occasional spot of light from Vila and, finally, as they flew farther out of range, the ack-ack stopped entirely. Charlie had not even bothered to turn on his searchlights.

"Watch for night-fighters," he told the gunner. He was beginning to feel tired. He brought his feet back from the rudder pedals and stretched his legs. He arched away from the back of the seat to relax the set muscles and noticed Choiseul at two-thirty. From this height it looked almost like a plateau. The New Zealanders flew over it every day, just a few feet above the tops of the trees. That way they could swing over and get a look at Buin Harbor in the daytime—a hell of a risky job. He thought of Vaughan flying the Hudson somewhere up ahead of them, and wondered how many planes the

Army was flying tonight. He rolled back the cuff of his flight suit and looked at his wrist watch. The big boys should be just a few miles this side of Fauro. By the time the TBFs were off Vella Lavella the 17s should be over Kahili.

The gunner spoke to him over the phones. "Mr. Lambert," he said, "there's something in the sky below us, sir."

Lambert took the phone from the panel. "How far away is it?"

"About three miles, sir."

"Keep your eyes on it. Let me know if it comes closer."

"Yes, sir."

Lambert wondered if it might be a night-fighter tailing them up to Kahili to spot their formation and speed and the way they split up for the attack. Sometimes the bastards got behind you and stayed there for hours at the same distance, and when you looked again they were gone. This one could wait off Choiseul in case any of the guys came limping home from Kahili.

He spoke to the gunner. "What's the story?" he asked.

"Don't know, sir," the gunner said.

"Do the others see him?"

"I think so, sir."

Lambert switched to Liaison. *"Knucklehead from Flint,"* he called. *"Knucklehead from Flint. Think Bogie following at seven thousand, distance three miles."*

"Roger," McRae's voice answered. *"Already reported. Look for him on the way home."*

Lambert turned and tried to look back, but he was strapped in too tightly. He faced ahead again. The hell with him, he thought. If he comes close, okay. Otherwise forget him. He reached down into his map pocket and brought out the Bougainville map. He held it so that it was illuminated by the moonlight and looked at the targets indicated on the Kahili area. Erventa Island was his, just inside the harbor, like an unsinkable anti-aircraft barge. Searchlights, too. He'd go up a few thousand higher and wait for the bastard to start shining his lights on the planes mining the harbor. Then—down we go, Buster, he thought. He folded the map and put it back into the big pocket below his knee.

There were clouds below him, blotting out the water, and the moon made them so bright that they looked almost like the white thunderheads over Henderson. They were not changing the way clouds did in a wind. He squinted his eyes to see what shapes he could find hidden in them, but they were too closely packed, like foam in a still picture or frozen surf. The clouds were dark where the moon did not touch them, the way the sea darkens away from the spray.

Lambert looked at the thirty-four torpedo-bombers around him, surging through the night toward the target ahead. They looked different than they did standing earthbound in their revetments. Thirty-five Avengers, body by Grumman, on their way to visit Charlie. He wished that there were a hundred more to go along. Well, here we come, Charlie, he said to himself—*F. O. B. Henderson*.

They were past the clouds that had blanketed the Slot, and, looking down, he saw the ribbon of moonlight that led to Kahili.

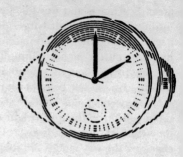

$\mathcal{F}$ORSYTH WAS BEGINNING TO FEEL TIRED. HE PULLED BACK THE hood a few inches and the cold air of the slipstream poured into the cockpit from both sides. He leaned forward toward the instrument panel so that the air would not strike his eyes. The cockpit grew cold quickly, and he filled his lungs and closed the hood again. He sat back, fully awake, and looked at the dim light of the compass at the top of the windshield. The plane was holding the course steadily. They were 5,000 feet above and to the right of Vella Lavella, but he could see its mists smoldering below, reaching up toward them like the wraiths of a thousand ghostly fires. The colors that the sun gave the islands by day were drawn away by the moon at night. When you went up the Slot in the daytime, there were the dark and light greens of the jungle and the shallows, the light gold of the sand, the bone-white of the exposed reefs and the changing blues of the water and the sky, but, at night, only the blues remained. Unless the moon were out to silver it, the water was black or gray and the clouds dark. The higher you were, the less color there was around you. At 15,000 the sky would be gray, pierced by a myriad of unwinking stars. Below, the colors would darken into a mottled gloom where sea merged with land almost indistinguishably.

He was glad his plane carried a torpedo. He loved the swooping gull dive and the skidding, full-flap run. Tonight he would come in from the west and level off over the land. That way the torpedo would be away before the ack-ack had a chance to throw much at him. He hoped Babe would do it the same way. It was a good idea for Colonel Sampson to talk things over with them before they got up to Kahili, but when you got there the barges or ships had always moved since the last recon photos and ack-ack sprang up out of nowhere and you had to size the thing up fast and figure the best way to do it. There was nobody to plan it for you again.

Eliot looked around and saw Babe's plane flying above him at eight o'clock. He took the phone from the panel and called Babe. *"Cricket from Cactus. Cricket from Cactus."*

"Cactus from Cricket. Go ahead."

"Follow me in," Forsyth said. His own words rattled harshly through his earphones. *"We'll start our run from the west."*

"Roger. Wilco."

Forsyth returned the phone to its clip and decided to switch to the main tank. He turned the fuel valve from auxiliary to main and the engine droned on without a sputter. His legs were getting tired and the weapons belt felt insupportably heavy. The .45 on his hip hung down heavily. Next time he'd tie the rawhide thong around his thigh to get it out of the way, or try a shoulder holster. He had never worn one because it always got in the way of the chute straps. Well, it wouldn't do much good to float down over Kahili. The Nips would pick you off before you landed or kill you on the ground. Maybe that was why Cordell always carried a Reising—to spray a landing space for himself.

He peered ahead over the cowl, trying to see Shortland in the distance, but there were only the bright moonlight path below and the gray dark sea beyond. In front of him, sparks shot down toward the water as a turret gunner warmed his guns. Little molten pellets fell from the tail as the radioman fired the thirty. He hoped that some day they'd put a fifty in the tail of each TBF. If a Zero got close enough to shoot at with the thirty, you were all through anyway. It was time to look for a place to sit down. . . .

He heard McRae's voice over his earphones. *"Shortland ahead. We'll bear north a little."*

Forsyth saw the plane ahead turn to the right and he followed, watching the compass swing to the new course.

When Lambert saw the others turning toward Bougainville Strait, he eased the throttle and called the other four planes that were carrying bombs. Looking around him he could see them above and behind him in formation, making a five-plane Vee—Williams and French, Brown and McIntyre.

"Egg-jockeys from Flint. Egg-jockeys from Flint. We'll orbit south of Fauro for about eight minutes until they get things started. Then: Williams to Pupukuna. French to Popatala. Brown to Aiaisina, and Mac, you take Kangu. I'll sit over Erventa. Take your time on the dive. Make sure the egg will hit. We haven't got enough to spare for practice runs."

"Okay, Ben," French said.

Ben switched to inter-com. "Pilot to gunners," he said. "We're almost there. Keep your eyes open on the way down and if I miss the light, see if you can shoot it out." He hung up the phone again.

The other planes had pulled ahead, over to the right. He saw them flying toward the tip of Choiseul and he wondered where the B-17s were. He looked over the side of the fuselage and saw Shortland on the left and Fauro to the right on the other side of the channel. Twenty miles beyond them lay Buin Harbor and Kahili airfield. He looked above through the mirror-like dome of the windshield to see if the B-17s were on their way back to Henderson. He pulled back his left cuff and looked at the dial of his wrist watch. Where the hell were they? He strained his eyes to look through the dark channel between Shortland and Fauro, but he could see no bomb flashes. There were no fires at Kahili yet. He wondered if they had gone up to Buka by mistake. Hell, no! A blind man could find his way to Kahili tonight. Even if there were new pilots and navigators on the strike, all they had to do was play follow-the-leader. The stars were out full blast, too. With your choice of a star-sight or an observed moon-altitude, how the hell could you get lost? He looked around the sky again for the Fortresses but there were only the moon and the stars and the planes that flew behind him. Then, as he looked ahead, he saw tiny spurts of light in the distance and he knew that the bombers were over their target. The explosions looked different from the ack-ack because they were wider and they ripped along in strings.

Lambert called the others on the radio. *"The big boys are over,"* he said, and looked toward the main body of TBFs, four miles away, off Choiseul. Soon, he knew, the planes would split into two groups—those with mines and those with torpedoes. As he flew closer, he could see the bombs bursting beyond Fauro, and the glow of little fires on the land.

He looked at the air-speed indicator and then at his wrist watch, figuring their dead-reckoning distance from Kahili. It was just about on the nose. Still, the B-17s had been a little late. He wondered if night-fighters had jumped them. Hell, that shouldn't make any difference.

He called the others again. *"Watch out for night-fighters,"* he said.

French's voice came over the phone. *"Right, Ben. We're watching your tail, but who the hell's gonna watch mine?"*

"Wake up your gunner," Ben said. *"The show's starting damn quick."*

They were close enough now to see ack-ack shooting up at the B-17s. The tracers joined the earth to the sky with little red tendrils that bent near the top and trailed away into the darkness. He could not see the Fortresses but he knew they must be at 20,000 feet, anyway. That high, chances for a hit were small; Charlie was not noted for accuracy.

Another string of bombs hit near the airstrip, tearing the darkness ahead into bursting flowers of light that faded and glowed and finally vanished. Still, no big fires had been started —if only they'd hit a fuel dump. He guessed that Charlie had hidden his gas on the hillside in caves above the airstrip, or sheltered it in camouflaged revetments. If a string went wild it might touch off something really big. It was good to knock out their planes on the ground and put holes in the runway, but tomorrow they'd shuttle down more planes from Buka and Kieta and tonight, after the strike was over, labor troops would start working on the airstrip, and by morning it would be almost as good as new.

He wondered how many planes would not return from the strike. If more than six were lost it would be considered unprofitable. It was strange how the war had come to be gauged by statistics—so many tons carried, so many miles flown, so many planes missing. Just figures—tons and miles and planes. That was the way you had to think about it. But the law of diminishing returns held good in the air, too, and every time you went on a strike, the chances of your return diminished. Forget it, he said to himself, the hell with that. . . .

Fauro was ahead and the thirty planes were somehow over the Strait. The ack-ack was still firing sporadically, but he could not see any bombs bursting, and the searchlights had not yet gone on. He wondered if any of them had been knocked out. Charlie probably knew his lights wouldn't reach as high as the bombers so he kept them dark. When they were on, you could photograph them and spot them for the next strike.

He spoke over the phone to the planes that were with him. *"Tally-ho, chaps,"* he said, with a broad accent. *"Let's head for Fauro."*

Lambert gave the plane a little right rudder and it turned smoothly, almost without lowering its right wing.

Williams' voice came over the radio. *"The Army's going home."*

Lambert looked up and saw the flight of Fortresses high above, to the right. They were flying high, so far away he could hardly see them. Their small black forms moved impassively through the night toward Henderson, their job finished. Another night, another strike, he thought. Let's get it over. . . .

Fauro was below and he banked gently to the right, so that the plane would make a wide circle over the island. He looked at his watch, and then to the left, toward the defensive area around the airfield. The ack-ack had stopped. A few fires flickered in the distance and he knew that they were probably planes that had been caught on the ground. Well, they didn't cost Charlie much—not with slave labor and stolen materials.

Looking back, he saw that the others were following him in the slow orbit. By the time we make the circle the others should be ready for business, he thought. He noticed how high the moon was—much brighter than when they started out. The air was bumpy over the island and he wondered if there was any ack-ack below. So far he had never noticed any, but there was always a first time. McRae must be getting ready to turn south soon.

Lambert decided to test the bomb doors. As they opened, he felt the rush of air fanning up against the loose legs of his flight suit. The plane shuddered as the resistance slowed it and he looked back and saw that French had opened his already. The warning light on the panel threw a diffused red glow over his hand on the stick. He could hear the hum of the motor that operated the doors shut off. The bay was open. He reached over and the doors began to close again. He might need the extra speed to get over to Erventa. The red light vanished and the green one shone from the panel. The hum of the motor stopped.

Ben looked at his watch again and at the darkness ahead where Kahili lay. Some of the fires had gone out but others flickered in the distance. If the planes had had empty fuel tanks they would not explode. Dummy planes would burn like that and Charlie built good dummies out of paper and canvas and wood. They looked real from the air and in the water, but if you spotted a plane in the same place two days in a row, the chances were it was a dummy and the hell with bothering to strafe it.

As he looked ahead, searchlights sprang up into the sky. Three beams waved back and forth against the dark background of the island and the clouds in the distance, losing themselves in the night above. Charlie must have heard McRae's gang. He waited for the first ack-ack to start, but it did not come. Another searchlight went up by Pupukuna Point.

He called Williams. *"There's yours,"* he said. *"See if you can put it out."*

"Wilco," Williams' voice answered. *"Quite a beam."*

As long as the searchlights pointed straight up, the others were safe. He knew they must be over the island now, dropping down toward the pass. The orbit was half finished. Fauro looked dark and lifeless below them. If he had to bail out it might be a good place to head for. He could probably hide out there for a while until he could make a dugout and head for Vella Lavella. Another searchlight beamed out from the left near Kangu. He watched it sweep the empty sky and called McIntyre. *"Looks like yours, Mac,"* he said. *"Maybe there'll be flak to go with it."*

"Hope so," Mac called back. *"Just as easy."*

There was no particular reason to have radio silence now. When they first came up, they always buttoned down their radios, but it didn't seem to make much difference any more. Charlie's snoopers could report you long before the airdrome could take a directional bearing on your radio frequencies. Ben looked at his watch again and then out of the side of the panel at the island below. The turn was lacking only ninety degrees. He hoped that the time had been figured right.

Back in the hills a battery of lights flashed up where he had never seen any before. They probed the sky uncertainly and he knew that the others must be getting close. Still there was no ack-ack. He glanced back at the planes and then called them.

"Open bomb doors," he said. *"We'll scoot over, in a minute."*

His mouth was going dry but he did not want to take time to get out his canteen. The little motor hummed beneath his feet and the diverted slipstream slashed up around his legs. The plane slowed as the doors opened out and he pushed the throttle ahead to even the speed.

The searchlights waved awkwardly ahead of them and he knew that the time was almost up. McRae must be almost at the pass. Then, out of the darkness, the ack-ack started popping wildly. The tracers went skyward and the shells exploded haphazardly above—not where McRae and the others were. They would come in where the zone of fire was least dense, do the job and get out . . . more mathematics and statistics. He hoped that he would never be killed by an error in figures.

As his plane finished its orbit, Lambert looked at his watch. He saw the others behind him and he straightened out and pushed the throttle all the way forward. He must be heading for Erventa now; it was almost in line with the airstrip. He saw the others catching up and closing the intervals between the planes. He put the stick over and back and the wings waggled. Then he pushed it forward an inch and the nose went down. The rush of wind under his legs grew as the air speed increased and the legs of his flight suit billowed out as they filled with the chilling wind. He watched the altimeter drop, and looked over the top of the cowl at the water below. There was an island inside the arc of his propeller, but he saw it was not Erventa. The ack-ack reached upward and the searchlights careened through the sky and then, as he looked ahead to the right of the naked airfield, he saw the first three planes come out of the dark hills heading for the harbor. The searchlights veered from the sky and groped for the speeding Vee and streams of flak fell toward the earth.

Lambert could see Erventa loom up out of the water ahead of him. He pushed the stick forward and felt his muscles tighten against the safety belt that dug into his stomach as the plane dropped down through the night.

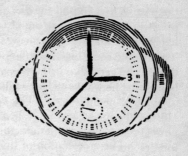

*H*E WAS NOT THINKING ABOUT THE OTHERS BEHIND HIM, breaking off to find their targets, nor of the planes caught in the lights as he looked at his altimeter and pulled back on the stick. He moved the flap lever and the plane slowed as they opened against the rush of air. The second Vee had come out of the hills and was dropping down toward the water. He looked at Erventa in the darkness below and banked sharply to the right. The plane was harder to handle with the bomb doors open and the flaps down and he gave it more rudder before straightening out.

The tracers leaped up over the harbor and he saw Williams' plane reach Pupukuna. He banked again and the nose dropped in a slow spiral. The palm of his left hand felt moist inside the cold leather glove as he reached for the bomb release. Then, as the third Vee of planes came over the beach, Erventa reached out toward them in a burst of flak and light. Ben pulled back the stick, and leaned forward to look into the sight. Then he pushed over in a steep, plummeting dive. The light in his sight was blinding, but he kept his eyes open. With the other eye he could see the air speed rising and the altimeter hand whirling around the dial. The battery below was firing steadily and he saw a string of tracers reach up lazily toward him like red beads on a string. The end of the string bent below him and faded into darkness, but another had sprung up and another and then the bowl of the searchlight seemed to fill the whole sight and he glanced quickly at the altimeter and pulled the bomb release. The nose of the plane surged up as the bomb left it and he pulled back hard on the stick and kicked the plane over to the right, away from the planes in the harbor. The acceleration of the plane stopped and he could feel the inertia pushing his body hard into the seat as though someone were standing on his shoulders, driving him down, crushing out his breath. He brought his head away from the sight and the lights dimmed as the blood was sucked away from his eyes. Then the pressure on his diaphragm ended and he sucked in a deep breath of air that filled his lungs and expanded the thoracic muscles. He straightened his shoulders and sat up in the cockpit. The terminal velocity had hunched him over in his seat until his head had almost touched the padded rim of the cowling. He breathed deeply again and felt his muscles relax. When the bomb doors closed, they cut off the torrent of wind that had been coming into the cockpit from below. His hands were beginning to sweat from the temperature of the lower altitude and he pulled down his goggles and slid the hood shut. Warm air filled the cockpit and he looked down at the searchlights on Erventa. The bomb should be almost there. Then, as he watched, the island seemed to blossom into a tremendous flaming blast that leaped high into the air and grew from the bottom until it spread and covered the island. The plane shook and he realized that his gunners were strafing. He turned back toward the billow of flame that was fading away and saw the tracers from the turret guns leap out through the blackness toward the dying glow of the island where the searchlights had been, toward the embers that burned in the darkness and flickered against the water of the harbor.

The Pupukuna light was out, but, as Ben looked, he saw a TBF blow up over Lamuai. It came apart fifty feet over the water and its pieces fell and plowed the surface into spray in the garish brilliance of the searchlights and the harbor fires. He looked to the left and saw a cargo ship burning, flames leaping over its masts. It was listing slightly and Lambert could see the great gap that the torpedo had left, extending up the side to the deck. More planes were coming out over the harbor and he saw two that had dropped their mines, climbing steeply above the searchlights that elevated to catch them.

Everywhere over Kahili and over the harbor, searchlights whirled and flak bursts crimsoned the night into sunset red. Another plane began its mine-laying run. Lambert watched it plummet down toward the harbor and saw the mine fall from its belly. Tracers from shore batteries followed it along and Ben waited for it to pull up and bank away, but it flew on and then, as the spray of tracers reached it, its right wing dropped and it slid down and struck the water in a huge spout that closed and surged over and he saw the tail stick up and then disappear, and he felt the tightness in his stomach and around his chest and when he looked away a searchlight caught his plane and there was a burst of flak near by that rocked him, and over him a plane headed away from the harbor. Ben pulled back the stick and turned right toward Pupukuna. He looked above for night-fighters, but only the incandescent moon streamed in through the clear dome, and, as he looked around, he saw that the searchlight had lost him. It waved up and down, searching the darkness futilely like the cane of a blind old man. He closed his eyes for a moment to rest them from the glare he had been watching and when he opened them he saw a plane falling over Kangu, side-slipping into a spin. It went over on its back slowly and when it hit the beach it exploded in a blast of white-hot flame. He could hear voices over his earphones now and he listened, but they all seemed to be talking at once, rapidly, with voices beyond their normal timbre, and then he heard Babe calling the rest of them.

"Cricket to Strike. Cricket to Strike. Tail shot away. Out of control. . . ."

Lambert looked across the sky past Kahili and saw Babe's plane spinning down into the lights. It hurtled earthward, falling brokenly, as it dropped faster toward the clearing beyond the airstrip. Ben felt his body stiffen as he watched it plummet the last hundred feet and detonate against the ground. Flames burst from it, lighting up the airstrip and Ben could see figures running away from the raging flames that soared up. Then another explosion geysered up and he banked away so that he would not have to watch. The main searchlights had been knocked out and Ben saw planes climbing under him, heading out toward the channel, and he pulled the stick back to gain altitude. They darted past him like fish in an aquarium window. A burst of flak jerked the nose up and he pushed the left rudder pedal to get away from the arc of fire. In the harbor the cargo ship burned, three barges flaming beside it. One had turned over on its side and, as he watched, it capsized and sank, the steam hissing high above it.

Babe's plane burned steadily on the runway and Ben looked beyond it to see if more planes would come out of the darkness, but they had all made their runs. He closed the hood and slid his goggles up on his forehead. He wondered why Babe had not tried to get out and whose planes the others had been. Ahead of him the planes were forming up. He pulled back the stick to climb to the homing altitude. Looking back over his shoulder, he saw that the ack-ack had stopped shooting and only a few searchlights seared the darkness below the moon. Ballale Island was below him and he knew that he was coming out the right way. He was glad that he had knocked out the stuff on Erventa. It was that battery in the hills that had crossed them up—that plus the heavy stuff on shore near the ships. Well, the ships had been scratched off in spite of them. He tried to think how many planes he had seen go down. One had blown apart over Lamuai. The second was shot down and crashed into the water after it had dropped its mine. The third had spun into the beach near Kangu, and Babe's plane had dropped onto the airstrip. Babe not coming back with them . . . not going up to Strike Command while Paul Scott quizzed them . . . not driving over to the mess hall in the early morning for coffee and pancakes. *Out of control,* Babe had said. The kid must have tried to bring it down because of the men. Christ! He had stayed with it, fighting for control all the way. *I hope he never knew when he hit,* Ben said, half aloud. Just a kid, too, not more than twenty—more likely nineteen. A wife somewhere in the States, parents, and next week a telegram to them from Washington. Ben felt bitterness rise. Why did the kids have to fight? Why not let the guys who'd lived their lives do the job? He pulled his weapons belt around and took out the canteen. The rough aluminum mouth felt cool against his lips and he drank almost half of the water without stopping. Then he replaced the cap and put away the canteen. He tried to count the number of planes ahead, but the leading ones were too far away and he could see only eight strung out above the Slot. He put his binoculars to his eyes and looked over the cowling, trying to read the fuselage numbers of the last planes. He turned and looked behind him to see if any planes followed him, but he could not see any.

He must have been the last to get out. It had been touch-and-go over the harbor. Babe and three others. He wondered who they were.

"Mr. Lambert," the turret gunner called, "there's a plane below us flying low over the water."

He took the phone from the panel. "Can you see what it is?"

"No, sir. Radioman can't make out what it is, either."

"We'll have a look." He pushed the stick ahead, gave the plane right rudder and dropped away in a whining dive. As it spiraled down, he saw the shadow above the water, a mile behind him. It looked too big to be a night-fighter, and, flying back toward it, he saw that it was a TBF limping home at 500 feet. He dropped toward it in a wide circle and switched to Liaison. Then he looked at it through his binoculars, trying to see its fuselage number. Focusing his glasses on it, he saw that it was shadowed by a cloud. He flew nearer and, when the plane came out of the shadow into the moonlight, he saw that it was Forsyth's plane. He pressed the speaking button on the phone.

"*Eliot,*" he said quickly, "*what the hell's the matter? Come on upstairs with the rest of us.*"

"*That you, Ben?*" Forsyth's voice crackled back. "*Afraid I can't. Part of my wing's gone.*"

Ben scanned Forsyth's plane and saw that almost all of the trailing edge of his right wing had been torn away. "*How the hell did that happen?*"

"*The usual way. The shore battery nicked me when I pulled up from my run. Main tank got it, too. Leaking like hell. Radioman killed.*"

"*Can you make it?*" Ben waited for the answer as he banked again to fly parallel with Forsyth. Then it came:

"*Don't think so, Ben. Not tonight.*"

At their low altitude Vella Lavella seemed to tower above

them to the right. Ben could see the little line of white where the waves rolled up against the narrow beach.

"How much gas have you got?"

"About sixty gallons. Must be a big rip in the tank."

Another voice broke in. *"Pipe to Flint. Pipe to Flint. Are you with us? Are you with us?"*

"Roger," Ben said. *"Affirm."*

"Get into formation, Ben. This is Weatherall in the lead."

"Eliot," Ben called, *"where's the skipper?"*

"Back there," Eliot's voice said. *"I saw his plane blow up."*

"Was that the first?"

"Yes."

God, Lambert thought, Larry gone! *"Who were the others?"*

"Joe Cordell and Williams."

Ben's hand dropped to his thigh and he looked up above into the empty sky, feeling terrifyingly lonely. His whole body felt cold as the names whirled around in his brain. Then he picked up the phone again.

"Eliot," he called, *"do you know who the fourth was?"*

There was a pause before Forsyth answered. This voice came anxiously over the phones: *"No, who was it?"*

"Babe. I heard him call out before he crashed."

"God," the phones said metallically. For a while Forsyth did not call again.

"Pipe to Flint. Pipe to Flint. Form up. Where are you? Form up."

"I'm flying at 500 with Forsyth."

"Is he in trouble?"

Forsyth's voice broke through. *"Not much, Ted, but just enough. Don't keep the coffee warm for me. I'll bring her down when she sputters."*

"Tough luck, Eliot. Stick with him, Ben, and see where he goes down."

"*Wilco,*" Ben said automatically.

"*See,*" Forsyth said. "*It's as easy as that. I'll just pull over to the curb and you drive on into town.*"

"*They'll send a Cat for you, boy.*"

"*Sure. Just like that.*"

Ben looked at the height of Kolombangara beside them, its peak stuck into the clouds at forty-five hundred. Sheets of mist seemed to curl up from its densely wooded slopes.

"*How'd you get out, Eliot?*"

"*Spotted Vaughan's flares. I was pretty well shaken up— didn't know where I was. Then I saw the light floating down in front of me. When I passed it there was another above me. I couldn't climb, so I waited until I found the course again.*"

"*Smart boy.*" Ben saw that they had passed the island and were flying slowly over Kula Gulf.

"*Ben.*"

"*Yes, Eliot.*"

"*Give Vaughan my share of the liquor, will you?*"

"*Certainly not.*"

"*I wish the skipper were going to be there to have a drink for me.*"

"*He didn't know he wasn't coming back,*" Ben said. "*None of them knew.*"

"*It's a funny feeling, Ben, sitting here watching the minutes go by while the gas leaks out. I haven't got much more.*"

"*Slide your hood back before you hit. Then get out fast. Might as well take off your chute now.*"

"*Right.*"

Ben looked at Forsyth's cockpit and saw the other's shoulders moving as he slid out of the harness. He looked up to see where the rest of the planes were, but there was only a dark layer of clouds above. The others were out of sight.

"*Ben.*"

"*Yes.*"

"*Will you take care of Babe's things for me? You know—get them together and all that.*"

"*Yes, Eliot.*" His throat felt suddenly taut.

"*And my stuff, too—in case something happens.*"

"*Nothing will happen.*"

"*Will you?*"

Ben did not answer for a moment. Then: "*Yes.*"

"*Good boy. I guess it's time to look for a likely spot.*"

"*Not yet, Eliot. Hang on a while.*"

"*Okay. Where do you suggest?*"

Ben thought for a moment. "*End of New Georgia,*" he said. "*Gatukai.*"

"*It's got an exotic name,*" Forsyth said, "*but it'll have to be closer than that.*"

"*Vangunu, then.*"

"*Reefs,*" Forsyth said. "*My little chart shows reefs.*"

"*Do you want to try landing on a beach?*"

"*No—I don't think so. They don't look good close-up.*"

They had passed Visuvisu Point and were flying parallel to New Georgia. Ben could see the water breaking over the reefs below, and the light gray of the offshore shallows. The clouds overhead were becoming more scattered and after a while the moon broke through, lighting the two planes that flew together over the sea.

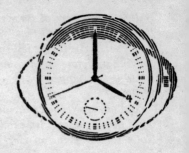

*W*ITH TWO-THIRDS OF ITS GAS GONE AND AN EMPTY BOMB bay, Ben's plane began to climb a little above Forsyth's. He trimmed the elevator tabs until the nose dropped to the horizon. Then he came down even with Eliot's plane again.

"Ben."

"Yes, Eliot."

"I can't think of anything funny to say. Do you know any jokes?"

"I can't remember any," Ben said.

He heard Eliot's gunner talking. Then another voice came over his earphones. *"Mr. Lambert, this is Thedford. Mr. Forsyth's gunner."*

"Yes, Thedford."

"I'd like to ask you to do a favor for me, sir—when you get back—if it won't be too much trouble."

"It won't be any trouble."

"Well, sir, if we don't get back by next week, I'd appreciate it if you wrote a little note to my mother and told her just how it happened. It'd make her feel a lot better. The address is in my ditty-box, sir, back in my tent."

"I won't have to," Ben said. *"You'll be back by then."*

"Will you do it, sir?"

"Yes, Thedford, I'll do it."

Forsyth's voice came through again. *"Might do the same for me, Ben."*

"Of course."

"Where are we now?"

Ben looked at the coastline to the right. It was growing darker now that the moon was fading at the end of the night.

"Looks like Vaholi Bay. Can't you make it to Russell?"

"Afraid not, Ben. This looks like the end of the line."

Ben heard the engine cough and then drone on as Forsyth bent over the wobble pump. He saw Forsyth straighten up in the cockpit and slide back the hood.

"That's all, Ben," he said simply. *"I think I'll start down now."*

"Wait . . ." Ben called, but Forsyth's plane had dropped away in a wide spiral toward the water and Ben knew that he was looking for a place to come down. He pushed the stick ahead and kicked his plane to the right, toward the looming outline of land above Vaholi Bay. Forsyth's plane was in a flat glide, its engine dead, heading toward the shallows off the beach. Its right wing dropped as it began to lose lifting power and then the plane was just over the water, near the shore, gliding beyond the surf line. Ben held his breath in the stillness of his cockpit as he watched it lose the last few yards of altitude. The low wing tip dipped into the black water first, sending up a thin line of spray that widened as the rest of the wing began to go in and then the plane had pivoted over the water, its right wing breaking off near the fuselage, and hurtled over on its back. A spout of water rose high above the widening circle of foam, and then dropped back to cover it. Ben dove his plane for the spot, and saw the left wing and part of the tail

emerge. While he watched he saw an object lighter than the rest bob up, clear of the sinking wreckage. It was a man in a yellow life jacket. Ben skimmed low over the water trying to see him, but the plane was moving too fast as he passed over the spot and the figure did not wave. Forsyth's plane disappeared and Ben saw the little figure floating listlessly toward shore, its head rolling to one side with the swell of the sea. Then it was too far behind him to see, and as he banked to go over again, he heard Weatherall calling him on the radio.

"Ben . . . Ben. What's happened to Forsyth? I can't reach him."

Ben took the phone from the panel wearily. "He's down," he said. *"He tried to stall in on Vaholi Bay but his wing was too badly shot up. Engine went dead before he could set her down."*

"Could you see anything?"

"Only one of them got out. The radioman was killed back at Kahili."

"Which one got out?"

"I don't know," Ben said slowly. *"He's unconscious in the water."*

"We're passing Russell now, Ben. Better come along."

"No," Ben said. *"I want to stick around for a while."*

"There's nothing you can do, Ben. Come on back."

"Is that an order?"

"Yes."

His plane passed over the spot where the yellow-jacketed figure drifted shoreward with the morning breeze.

"Roger," he said. *"Roger, Wilco."*

He banked to the right again and began to climb above the level of the island jungle, watching his compass until he had swung to the homeward course. The moon had gone out of the sky, and as he rose above the light clouds, he closed the hood and leaned back against the headrest. His body felt almost without energy and he was thirsty, but he did not want to get out the canteen again. Ordinarily he would be taking the waxed K-Ration from his breast pocket, but this morning he was too tired. The clouds thinned, and when he reached 3,000 feet, he leveled off and saw Russell Island ahead in the gray morning light. He looked at his watch and realized that the sun would be coming up in a little while.

Suddenly Ben began to feel cold and he wondered if a malaria chill was starting. He had seen Cordell's bunk, wet through with his sweat when he dressed for the strike, and knew that Joe had got another chill while he was away playing poker. Maybe another one had hit him tonight, Ben thought. Maybe he took so many yellow pills that the stuff made him dopey. It could have happened that way. He would mail Joe's letter tomorrow. In the afternoon he would pack Joe's things into his sea chest to go home on the next Liberty ship that went back to the States—not much to remember him by. And there was Larry's big bottle. The squadron ought to keep it and take it with them wherever they went. After a while there would be nobody left who knew where the bottle came from or who had ever heard of Larry McRae or Torpedo Eleven.

The pictures of the lights, and the planes spinning and crashing, and the ack-ack and the glare of the burning ships, kaleidoscoped through his mind. It had all started so easily with the first string of bombs the Army had dropped, and then the searchlights waved around and the ack-ack came up and then everything had fused together in a hell of noise and light and explosions, and tapered off gradually until now he was flying home alone, with Russell just ahead and only the easy throb of his engine to remind him of things he was flying from.

His eyelids felt heavy and he fought against the desire to

close them. He had been without sleep for a long time. When he finally landed and went through the Intelligence quiz at Strike Command, he'd have a cup of coffee and turn in for the day. He slid back the hood again so that the cold air would keep him awake, and he saw a light patch forming above the dark gray horizon where the sun would come up. He looked above at the sky and saw that the stars had gone out. The moon was paling quickly, robbed of its yellow light by the gray morning sky.

As he flew over the airstrip at Russell, he saw three men walking across the runway toward some fighters at the side of the strip. Probably crewmen getting ready to fuel the planes for an early patrol over Santa Isabel; the pilots would have another half hour's sleep. Ben wondered if there would be another strike soon—not Kahili for a while. Maybe they'd start working on Rekata or concentrate on Munda or Vila. Kahili would be no good to Charlie while the mines kept out his gas barges. The squadron might get leave before the next operation, but there was nobody he wanted to go on leave with this time; he'd better plan on seeing Ann in Sydney. It would be good to see her again—keep his mind off the others.

In the distance, he could see the low gray tip of Cape Esperance with Savo to the left. There was a thin bank of fog over the water that gave him a false sense of altitude, as though he were really high. He watched it roll by, underneath the wings, driven by the offshore breeze, feeling as though the plane were standing still above the gray-white fog, rolling along on a huge conveyor belt. His eyelids started to close and he shook himself and opened his eyes wide. He was still cold, but now he knew the chill was not coming and he left the hood open, so that he could breathe the cold air that tore across his cheeks and lips.

The outline of Guadal was a little higher and he could see

Savo more clearly. He looked across the sky for the other planes, and when he did not see them, he knew they must be coming in on another course, farther to the west. He picked up the phone and called Henderson.

"Flint to Tower. Flint to Tower. Come in. Come in."

Static crackled over his earphones for a moment until he heard the control officer's voice.

"Flint from Tower. Flint from Tower. Go ahead."

"Esperance bearing zero-seven-oh. Esperance bearing zero-seven-oh."

"Very well. Are there any others after you?"

"No," Ben said. *"I'm the last."*

"Are you in trouble?"

"No. I'm all right."

"Any fighters jump you on the way back?"

"No," Ben said. *"Uneventful return. No interception."*

"Slight cross-wind this morning from Northeast."

"Okay," Ben said and clicked the phone back into place.

He would pack Babe's gear in the evening when he could be alone—the moldy uniforms he had brought along and some of the souvenirs he had got yesterday and the khakis he had scrubbed in the morning. His wife's address would be somewhere around the tent, maybe on a letter. He would not pack Eliot's for a while, though—not until there was no more hope of his coming back. Then he would have to write the gunner's mother the way he had promised. Dear Mrs. Thedford: I know that no words can suffice to diminish your grief at the loss of your son but it may well make you proud to know the heroic way he died. . . . Hell, that was wrong. It'd have to start some other way. No sense in telling her how much she missed him or how shocked she was at his death; she knew that better than you could ever tell her. And yet you couldn't just say that you were flying alongside his plane when he called you on the radio before he died, and said please write mother. . . .

The shore of Guadal was turning black slowly and beyond it, on the horizon, the patch of light gray was widening and growing brighter in the center. Behind him, the moon looked white against the colorless sky, like a half-round cloud that would change shape in a moment and vanish.

He wondered where Larry's gear would go; he had no wife or mother and Ben did not know where his father lived, if he was still alive. Well, the Squadron could send a dispatch to Washington and ask about it there. They had all the answers in Washington. . . .

Ben could see Vaughan's Hudson flying slowly toward Henderson. The other planes had passed it, leaving their guide behind, now that there was light. He thought of calling Vaughan on the radio but realized he'd be busy giving weather reports or talking with the Tower before coming in. The Hudson flew at a steady 5,000, methodically, like a robot-plane, radio-controlled from the ground. In the afternoon it would be flying again and perhaps at night, too, if there was another strike.

His cheeks seemed to have lost all feeling from the constant force of the wind against them. He touched them with his gloved hand and pinched them until he could feel a little pain. His legs were beginning to feel dead from the hips down and he knew that the all-night pressure on the end of his spine was blocking circulation and shutting off nerve sensation. He tried wiggling his toes, but it was too much of an effort and he brought back his feet from the rudder pedals and moved his legs at the knees until the torque of the propeller made the plane start to turn and he pushed his feet forward and brought the plane back to the course. He did not bother to look at the compass when he saw Kokumbona rising out of the jungled hills. Below him at the left, the first of the beached transports lay on its side as the waves broke around its rusted stern. Then he could see the next one beyond the point, and turning to the right he saw Fighter Two standing starkly out of the gray plantation, and beyond it, Henderson.

He brought up his binoculars and looked above the far end of Henderson. The TBFs were orbiting, waiting to land. He dropped the binoculars and turned the plane to the left, heading toward Lunga Point on the long leg of a triangle that would bring him to the east end of Henderson by the time it was his turn to land. Ben eased the throttle and the plane slowed as he passed over Lunga Beach, heading toward Florida Island. He could see Tulagi Harbor and Gavutu and Tanambogo and, in the distance, Malaita.

Ben began to think about Kahili, but took his mind away from it as he watched the sky lighten in the east. When he looked around, he saw Vaughan's Hudson plodding toward the far end of Henderson Field, where it would circle with the others before dropping down for a landing. He thought again of calling him, but he was too tired to hold the phone. His lips were parched and his chest felt constricted. He straightened his back against the padding of the chute and felt it give easily against his pressure. It made him feel better and he sat erect for a while before he slumped again. He hoped he would be able to go to the tent quickly and fall asleep. He had never felt so tired in his life, and there was a twinge in his thigh from the old bullet scar. It was getting white now but it would be a long time before it tanned like the rest of his body.

He banked the plane to the right and headed back toward the shore of Guadalcanal. The cold mists seemed to simmer up from the jungle, up toward the evenly spaced Grummans that looked as though they were sliding steeply down a wire toward the airstrip. His plane leveled off, and now it was heading toward Fighter One. Only three TBFs were left above the end of Henderson and one of them banked sharply and lost altitude as it started to come in for a landing. He watched it lose speed and saw its wheels fold down awkwardly until they were vertical, jutting from under its wing like the thin legs of a hawk. The plane sideslipped a little and lost altitude quickly over the palms and he saw it sway from side to side, fishtailing before it straightened just above the edge of the runway. Another plane was following it and when its wheels began to unfold, the last one banked away and came back, spiraling down after the second. Ben pulled down his goggles and looked over the side of his plane. He was above the jungle now, heading toward the end of the fighter strip. He turned a little to the right and called the Tower.

"*Tower from Flint. Tower from Flint. Permission to land.*"

"*Come in any time. Runway's clear.*"

Ben pushed the stick ahead, watching the altimeter drop until it had reached 600. Then as he released the wheels, he felt the plane shudder and he banked hard to the right again before he leveled off. The landing gear locked and the warning light went on. Ben felt the plane vibrate again and slow as the flaps opened. He looked at his air speed and pushed the nose down. The controls were slack and he had to move them exaggeratedly as the air speed fell. He eased the throttle more and the engine began backfiring. He pushed the mixture indicator ahead to *Rich* and looked over the cowl at the runway ahead. The plane was dropping too fast and he pulled back the stick and the nose came up again. He was in line with the landing strip and as the engine idled he could hear the air whistling over his flaps.

Ahead of him, the runway was clear. The last TBF had reached the far end and was turning off toward the taxi airstrip. He could see the palm trees clearly as his plane glided above them, and then he was over the edge of the runway and the matting rose toward him and he pulled back the stick and the plane dropped lightly to the earth. It rolled along the uneven mat rapidly and he braked it at intervals until the tail wheel was down and then he put the brakes on hard and the plane slowed as it rolled toward the end of the runway.

Ben Lambert pushed up his goggles and looked across the width of the strip. Dust was swirling behind a file of planes bumping along toward the east end of Henderson. When his plane came to a stop he pushed the throttle ahead and turned off the end of the landing mat, onto the taxi strip. As his plane moved slowly over the rough lane, he heard behind him the sound of a plane taking off.

He looked around at the early morning sun gilding the tops of the palms, and an SBD roared overhead. He watched its wheels folding away as it banked to the west, flying on the morning strike at Munda.

The sun of the South Pacific came up slowly over the eastern tip of Guadalcanal in the Solomons. Its warm light touched the coral reefs and shallows of the little bays offshore . . . its rays moving . . . until they lighted the end of the bomber strip at Henderson Field.

As the sun warmed the jungle, it killed the mists that had clung to it during the night . . . and the birds shrieked their protests as they flew from tree to tree, trying to escape the coming of the day.

The clouds that had hung low over Kokumbona, smothering its hills in layers of mist, retreated upward, leaving below . . . a cool, heavy dew. Sealark Channel . . . swelled a little as the tide began to change, glittering back at the pale morning sky.